# POSSOONS

*stories*

# POSSOONS

## *stories*

## Rachelle Rogers

InWordBound
p r e s s

Asheville, North Carolina

*for the Muses*
*in all their incarnations*

# ACKNOWLEDGMENTS

Some of the stories in this collection have been previously published. "Rethinking Max" first appeared in *WNC Woman*. "Restoration" was first published in *Cezanne's Carrot*, and subsequently became integrated into the novel, *A Love Apart*. "Why Stefan had to rent a sander and refinish the floors in Brenda's Bedroom" first appeared in *Flashquake*, and was later reprinted in *Shaking Like A Mountain*. "The Impermanence of Eagles" first appeared in *Pointed Circle*.

"Not About Tahiti" and "Possoons" received Honorable Mention in The Black Mountain Center for the Arts short story competition. "Harry Meets The Goddess" was awarded a prize in The Writers Workshop short story competition.

To love is to suffer. To avoid suffering, one must not love. But, then one suffers from not loving. Therefore, to love is to suffer, not to love is to suffer, to suffer is to suffer. To be happy is to love. To be happy, then, is to suffer, but suffering makes one unhappy. Therefore, to be unhappy one must love, or love to suffer, or suffer from too much happiness—*I hope you're getting this down.* —Woody Allen, *Love and Death*

# CONTENTS

# NOT ABOUT TAHITI

Eva couldn't resist the giant Philodendron she saw at The Home Depot. It had sprawling stalks and ten inch fingers. It made her feel tropical, like she was bringing home a little piece of paradise. Eva placed the plant on a stool in the entrance foyer, right beside the brass coat rack. She named it Phil. She wondered if her husband, Alvin, would even notice it.

Hawaii, Tahiti, Bora Bora—Eva had always dreamed of exotic places. She collected brochures and maps, showed them to Alvin. All he'd say was, "I'm not going any place that looks like a fly speck in the middle of fifteen inches of ocean." But Eva didn't give up. She taped photos to the bathroom mirror— floating lotus blossoms on clear pools, unspoiled lagoons, beaches melting into aquamarine sea. Not like the edge of the

Atlantic that lapped at Fort Lauderdale. That ocean was murky and polluted. Tar washed up on its shore. Eva had stepped in it more than once and hadn't been able to get it off her feet for weeks.

Alvin opened the front door. Eva watched him, undetected, from the kitchen archway as the new tangle of plant attacked him. "What the hell...?" he said, then shoved aside its groping hands and hung up his jacket. A minute later, as if he'd noticed nothing unusual, Alvin mumbled "I'm home," walked into the living room and collapsed into his recliner with the newspaper.

Eva approached him. She was barefooted, her recently highlighted hair pulled into a chignon, a pink hibiscus fastened behind her ear. She wore a sarong with magenta and white flowers on it, cupped by green leaves. She felt like she'd stepped out of a painting by Gauguin. Eva waited for Alvin to look at her. Finally, he shifted his eyes toward where she was standing.

"Don't you think you're a little old to dress like that?" Alvin said.

"I'm not *old*." Although she'd recently turned sixty, inside, Eva still felt forty. It was funny how that happened, how, on the inside, she could feel her best age, like she hadn't moved beyond its beauty and desires. Yet when she looked in the mirror, how betrayed she could feel by the outside sags, bags and wrinkles of time.

Alvin returned to reading his paper.

I'm sick and tired of being treated like I don't exist, Eva thought, like I don't matter. But this time, she didn't say a word. When it came to Alvin, words were a waste of energy. Instead, she dumped the Tropical Mango Chicken she'd spent all afternoon preparing down the disposal and listened to it grind her efforts to mush.

"What's for dinner?" Alvin called from the living room.

"Nothing. I tossed it down the sink."

That, plus the uneven growl of a motor got Alvin's attention. He rushed into the kitchen, pages of news unraveling in his trail. "You'll mess up the whole mechanism. And if you don't put baking soda in that drain, it'll stink."

Eva thought things already stank.

It hadn't always been that way. Or maybe it had, and it was only that lately Eva felt she'd reached her limit. Women her age often did. Something happened to a woman after menopause. She might paste banners to her rear car bumper exclaiming *I'm out of estrogen and I've got a gun.* She might watch *Shirley Valentine*, *Fried Green Tomatoes*, and, in Eva's case, *South Pacific* maybe fifty times. Suddenly, she might not care a hoot how she appeared to others, not even her husband—particularly not her husband—only how true she was to herself, and there was no telling where that might lead.

"You'll have to fix your own dinner tonight, Alvin." Never in thirty-two years of marriage had Eva used those words, yet her voice was calm and certain.

Alvin stared at her like a child with a boo-boo expecting her to fix it, but Eva was tired of being Alvin's Band-Aid.

"There are eggs," she said. "And cheese. You can make yourself an omelet. I'm going out."

Alvin stood, slack-jawed and slump-shouldered, in the

middle of the kitchen, the bulge above his disappearing waistline even more exaggerated. Eva fought the impulse to help him out of his misery. She took a breath, sighed, then headed for the bedroom to put on sandals and a sweater. When she came back, Alvin hadn't budged.

"Didn't you hear me? You're on your own tonight."

"If you think this tantrum is going to get you to some South Sea island, you can think again."

"This is not a tantrum, and I know better than to think it will get me anywhere. Now, if you don't mind, I'm leaving."


This was a new experience for Eva, this walking out at dinnertime in a sarong. She wasn't sure where to go. It's a lovely evening, she thought. I'll drive up to Amanda's. Amanda was Eva and Alvin's daughter. Because no one had nurtured Eva's dreams, Eva had worked hard to nurture Amanda's desire to become an architect.

When she pulled up, Eva heard her two granddaughters, Annie and Michaela, arguing out back. She opened the wrought iron side gate and went around to where they were sitting in the shade of the covered patio.

Michaela waved. "Hi, Gram."

Annie slouched in a chair, arms crossed, a pout on her lips. "Michaela's being mean to me, Grammy."

"I am not," Michaela said.

"Okay, my beauty girls. That's enough." Eva went over and kissed each of them. "Where's Mommy?"

"Inside," Michaela said.

Amanda rushed out. "Ma, what's wrong? You never come without calling."

"Nothing. Nothing's wrong."

"Is Daddy with you?"

"No.

"Are you still arguing about Tahiti?"

"I'm trying a new approach," Eva said.

Amanda put the napkins, placemats and utensils she was carrying on the patio table. She perused Eva's sarong. "I see."

"You don't like it?"

"Actually, I do." Amanda straightened the hibiscus in Eva's hair. "Very exotic."

"I like it, too," Michaela chimed in. "The flowers are pretty, Gram."

"Thank you, sweethearts."

Eva began to arrange the place settings.

"I dumped the Tropical Mango Chicken I made down the disposal," she said. "I told your father he could fix his own dinner."

"Mother, you didn't!"

"I did."

"Is he all right?"

"He'll survive."

"Does he know you're here?"

"I don't have to report to him."

"I'll call and tell him. Ben will be home shortly. You'll eat with us, okay?"

"If it's not too much trouble."

Amanda gave Eva a don't-be-ridiculous look, then turned to Michaela. "Come with me and I'll give you another setting for Gram?"

Eva didn't stop Amanda from calling Alvin, but she had no intention of talking to him herself.

"So what did your father say?"

"He tried to pretend everything was just hunky dory."

"I rest my case."


Eva decided the Philodendron looked lonely by itself in the foyer, so she stopped at The Home Depot and found an Aspidistra to keep it company. She only intended to buy that one plant, but got lured to the Areca and bamboo palms on sale, and the large Dracaena marginata with its shiny clusters of skinny green leaves edged in red.

When she got home, she introduced the Aspidistra to Phil in the foyer, and placed the palms and Dracaena in a sunny corner a few feet behind Alvin's recliner, next to the peace lily Amanda had given her. The large plants made a lush arrangement. Eva sang as she watered them. *Bali Ha'i is calling, where the sky meets the sea, here am I your special island, come to me, come to me…*

That evening, Eva had her Yoga for Eternal Youth class with her best friend Rose, and their new friend Dottie, sixty-two, a former "flower child" from San Francisco. Dottie had dubbed them The New Sixties (as in age, not decade) Revolution.

Afterwards, Dottie told Eva and Rose about Cassadaga, a tiny town in central Florida known for its psychic readers.

"I'm game," Eva replied, surprising herself.

"Me, too," Rose seconded.

So they made a plan to drive up the next weekend.


Eva couldn't remember the last time she'd taken an overnight trip with girlfriends. Maybe never. And she didn't know when she'd had so much fun. They took turns driving as she, Rose and Dottie laughed themselves silly over everything. "Three men at one time?" Eva said, blushing. She couldn't imagine it. Her wildest sex was the New Year's Eve she and Alvin had gone to a boring party and wound up "doing it" on their neighbor's bathroom floor.

Cassadaga was nothing like Eva expected. The hundred year old town had only a dozen or so streets lined with small, two-story cottages, lush lawns and old oaks. Simple, handmade shingles advertised "Certified Medium," "Psychic Healer," "Spiritual Counselor." The town had a Spanish-style hotel and the Colby Memorial Temple erected in homage to its founder, but no grocery store or gas station or bank.

Dottie had made appointments for each of them in advance with different psychic readers. They arranged to meet afterwards at the bookstore. Dottie directed Eva to a small blue cottage where she was greeted by a fifty-ish, anorexic-looking woman named Astara with frizzy brown hair and enough turquoise jewelry to double her weight.

"Most of our readers prefer no interruptions," Astara explained, "but with me you can ask questions along the way."

"Okay," Eva said. She crossed her legs.

Astara picked up a pale pink crystal from a table next to her and clutched it in her right hand. "Your deceased mother is around you very strongly," Astara began. "She says to tell you she understands, and not to give up, that there's a surprise in store very shortly."

Eva tried to keep an open mind. "Does she say what kind of surprise?"

"She says… " Astara paused, "lights, it has to do with lights."

"Hmmm."

Astara then got into specifics she couldn't possibly have known on her own—how pained Eva still was over the rift her sister had instigated between them years before; how Eva had miscarried a second child; how she'd regretted not going back to finish her degree after Amanda had been old enough.

"I see flowers around you," Astara continued, "tropical flowers."

"I have lots of plants in my house." Eva held back tears. "My husband, Alvin, doesn't even notice."

"He can be stubborn," Astara said, giving Eva's hand a sympathetic pat.

"You've got that right." Eva wondered whether Dottie might have clued Astara in on Alvin.

"You've had at least five lifetimes in the Polynesian Islands."

"Five?" Eva said. "You don't say."

"At least." Astara closed her eyes again. Her eyeballs shifted from right to left to right under their lids, as if she was scanning for inside information. "Only one with your current husband."

"I've had other husbands?"

"Oh yes."

Eva let the idea of being married to someone other than Alvin roll around her mind. It made her dizzy.

"I've been trying to convince Alvin to take a vacation to someplace exotic," Eva said. "Hawaii maybe, or Tahiti, but he's not interested."

"I'm not surprised."

"You're not?"

"In a past life he drowned off the coast of Bora Bora on a fishing boat that got blown out to sea in a storm. It was very frightening, and part of him remembers."

Eva hadn't considered other lifetimes, yet she'd always felt drawn to the South Seas. Now she'd even taken to wearing sarongs and filling her living room with tropical plants. And it was true Alvin never wanted to go into the ocean past his knees, that he seemed afraid of tiny tufts of land surrounded by miles and miles of nothing but water. All of this was at least something to think about.

"Do you see that Alvin will ever change his mind about taking me on vacation?"

"To the South Seas?" Astara shook her head. "Not likely."


When Eva got home from her weekend with The New

Sixties Revolution, Alvin was right where she'd left him—in his recliner in front of the TV, this time watching a "Star Trek" re-run.

"So?" he said, without looking up.

"So, what?"

"Did you have your tea leaves read?"

"I lived five past lives in Polynesia."

Alvin turned toward Eva. "Then you've been there already."


Eva craved color to offset her lush living room foliage. Potted orchids would be just the thing. She set out early and spent the morning at Potted Paradise, The Orchidarium and Fogelman's Exotic Plants in search of them. They were more expensive than she'd expected. You deserve a little extravagance, she told herself. You only live once. She chuckled at the thought. She knew Dottie and Astara would disagree.

Eva eventually decided on a pink passion Phalaenopsis with its elegant spray of blooms, a lacy purple Dendrobium, a yellow Cymbidium, and Queen of the Orchids, a ruffled white Cattleya. They smelled heavenly. Each came in its own glazed ceramic container. She added a hanging Fuchsia that caught her eye with its profuse cascade of magenta and purple blossoms. Perfect for in front of the window.

Eva spent hours finding the right placement for her sumptuous garden. She hung the Fuchsia from a white bracket above the middle of the picture window, and mixed the orchids in among the palms. Some pots she rested on the floor, others she raised onto a set of small stacking tables. She switched and shuffled until the whole arrangement looked just right. "Oh, you are all so beautiful," she crooned.

When he came home, Alvin didn't say a word about the fact his recliner nested in the middle of a tropical paradise.

"I made dinner tonight, Alvin." Eva was so pleased with her orchids, she'd felt in a generous mood. "Roast chicken with those little red potatoes you like."

Alvin looked at her. She detected the hint of a smile.

"Aren't you going to talk to me?" she said.

"I have nothing to say."

"Don't you think the flowers are lovely?"

"I don't know what to think anymore."

The phone rang and Alvin jumped to answer it. He had only been on a minute, when Eva heard him say, "Me, too," then hang up.

"Amanda," he explained. "She's coming by to pick up Michaela's bicycle."

Amanda arrived as Eva and Alvin were finishing dinner. "These flowers are gorgeous!" she said, as she entered the living room.

Eva glared at Alvin. "See?"

Amanda hugged Alvin, then Eva. She joined them at the dining room table. "But don't you think you've gone just a little overboard, Ma?"

"See!" Alvin said.

"Are you siding with your father, Amanda?".

"I'm not siding with anyone." Amanda looked concerned.

11

"Is this still about Tahiti?"

No, Eva thought. It never really was. "Who cares about Tahiti?" she said.

"Who cares about Tahiti!" Alvin shouted. "You turn the living room into some kind of tropical jungle, and you're telling me this isn't about Tahiti?"

Eva turned to Amanda. "Do you want some roast chicken?"

"No, thanks." Amanda's eyes shifted from Eva to Alvin. "What's going on with you two?"

"You know, Alvin, I've had other husbands," Eva said.

Alvin nearly choked on the chicken bone he'd been nibbling. "What are you talking about?"

"And I happen to know that in another lifetime you drowned in a fishing boat off the coast of Bora Bora."

Alvin glared into space as if some distant memory beckoned him, but Amanda's voice seemed to interrupt his reverie.

"Mother, will you please tell me what's going on?"

A tangle of emotion knotted in Eva's chest.

"Coffee's ready," she said. She got up and headed for the kitchen. Amanda, then Alvin followed her.

"What's going on," Eva gushed, "is thirty-two years of marriage to your father. She began to weep as she opened the cupboard, pulled three mugs from a shelf and slammed the door. Scooping spoons from a drawer, Eva clanged them onto a serving tray next to the mugs. She pulled a tissue from her pocket and blew her nose. "He's never taken the time to know me for who I am."

Alvin's lips separated as if he might have something to say, but nothing came out.

Eva grabbed the tray and headed back to the dining room table. Amanda followed with the carafe of coffee and a plate of apple Danish, Alvin behind her.

"I don't think Daddy feels that way." Amanda poured the coffee and handed Alvin a mug. "Do you, Daddy?"

"He's stubborn," Eva said.

"Not stubborn," Alvin mumbled.

Eva stared at him. "What would you call it?" She cut a Danish in half and put a portion on her plate. High emotion made her crave sweets.

"Not stubborn," Alvin repeated, examining his coffee as if he saw a fly floating in it. "Afraid."

Eva's mouth, full of chewed pastry, hung open. That was the last response she'd expected.

"Of what, Daddy?" Amanda took Alvin's hand the way she always did when they were having a serious talk.

For a moment, Eva felt jealous of her own daughter.

Alvin spoke softly, addressing only Amanda, as if he was embarrassed for Eva to see him so vulnerable.

"Afraid your mother will outgrow me, stop loving me. That I'll wake up one morning and she'll be gone."

Eva sprang from her chair and rushed into the living room toward her little corner of paradise. She blotted a tear, pinched two brown leaves from the bottom of a palm, traced new blooms along an arm of orchid. She thought of her mother, of how she was told her mother understood and not to give up. "A surprise," Astara had said. "Lights." So far, things still looked pretty dim and Eva's patience was running thin.

Eva heard Amanda's car start up in the driveway. A minute later, Alvin shuffled toward her.

"It's happening, Evie. You have new friends, you go to see foreign films, you have your palms read, you sing to your plants. You look happy all the time." Alvin pushed wisps of hair back from his forehead with the flat of his hand. "And beautiful."

It had been ages since Alvin had given Eva a compliment. She felt her heart soften.

"I know you think I've been acting crazy lately," she said, "but I have to tell you, Alvin, it feels good. I like this new me. I've discovered I'm an interesting person. And funny, too."

Alvin looked wistful. "You always were."

"I can't go back to the old me. You do understand that, don't you?"

Alvin didn't answer. He began to walk away, then paused. "I have something to show you, Evie." He left and returned with an envelope. "I was waiting for the right time."

"What is it?"

"I've been thinking maybe we do need a vacation."

Eva eyed him cautiously. What was he up to? The last time Alvin had suggested a vacation, it had been a car trip to Connecticut to visit his sister Paula and her two yelping, squish-faced, ankle-biting dogs, Tutti and Fruitti. "What did you have in mind?" she said.

Alvin pulled a brochure out of the envelope and handed it to Eva. At least it couldn't be Connecticut, she thought.

"It's not Tahiti, Ev…"

"Then I'm not interested," she said. But a moment later, Eva thought perhaps she was being too harsh. Never before had Alvin taken the initiative in anything.

Slowly Eva lowered her gaze. In front of her she saw a dazzling night photo of…Paris.

"Of course," she whispered, tears blurring her new vision. "Lights. The City of Light." It wasn't Tahiti, but Alvin had done good. "Oh, Alvin," she said, kissing him on the cheek. Bright possibilities already drifted through her mind. She thought about the Louvre. About Monet. About the gardens at Giverny. About all those water lilies.

# RESTORATION

Unable to sleep, Julian shifted from side to side poking angles of himself through the covers. He'd only recently moved to the mountains of North Carolina and the haunting of owls and screeching drone of cicadas disturbed him more than the city traffic had outside his Upper West Side apartment.

When Sam was alive, New York seemed the ideal place to live. Museums, theater, ballet, great restaurants, good friends—they'd shared these things for nine years. "He was remarkable," Julian heard himself say so often in the last months. "Even when the cancer had gotten the best of his body, Sam never let it destroy his spirit."

It was ten months since Sam's death, ten months since Julian last touched brush to canvas. Without his art, sleep became shallow, agitated, dreams disappeared. And everywhere Julian turned, Sam was missing. He was missing from the breakfast table with his dark, tousled hair and soulful eyes, attempting to smile through the remnants of a late evening of champagne and museum fundraising. He was missing from Julian's bed when he reached for him in the night, when a slant of light illuminated the now empty place where they'd once held each other's dreams. He was missing in a vacant toothbrush slot, the glaring order of a desk, the ten thousand things that wore his imprint in a home and in a life.

For weeks after Sam's cremation, Julian ate meals out, and more often than not, let himself fall asleep on the living room sofa, where he'd remained until morning. The memory of Sam's frail body, the same body that had once navigated the slopes of Aspen, filled Julian with impossible grief. Over and over, he relived those last hours by his lover's side, his hand wrapped around Sam's bony fingers struggling to let him go. A tightness took up permanent residence in the hollow of Julian's chest, magnifying the guilt he felt for every breath.

Julian lay in the dark, trailing shadows, stroking the miniature gold key he wore around his neck. Sam had given it to him the night they'd moved in together. They'd first met two months earlier at a Soho gallery. Tired from painting, Julian had debated whether or not to attend his friend CJ's opening, yet a sense of something important cajoled him into going. When he'd arrived, he was immediately drawn to a man with dark hair standing alone, studying a painting. Several inches shy of Julian's six feet, he wore a black jacket over blue jeans and a black silk shirt. He seemed a few years older than Julian's thirty-one.

*Who are you?* Julian formed the thought and launched it on a mental wave. Slowly, the man turned, a look of concentration on his face as if he thought he'd heard someone call to him faintly or from a distance. He smiled and walked toward Julian. "Sam Keaton," he said. Julian noticed Sam's eyes were different colors—one blue, one hazel flecked with yellow. He wondered if he saw the world through a broader spectrum. Together they gazed at the canvas in front of them. Like the moment, the painting, too, was surreal—a maze of black and white passages with a tiny gold key shining at its center. "The key is everything," Sam had said.

With Sam's death, Julian realized he didn't know himself apart from their relationship. Even his art, he admitted, wasn't pure, but had often been calculated to please his lover. Not that it had to. Although, what Sam, as a curator for the Museum of Modern Art and himself a fine painter, thought of Julian's work mattered to Julian. Perhaps too much, and the feeling of being estranged from his own authenticity tugged at him.

Why am I so afraid to look inside my own skin? Julian had thought in a courageous moment. But too distraught to search further, he'd drowned his questions in the cacophony of a busy life, hidden his pain beneath a spurious fазаde appearing as solid as Da Vinci, when, slippery as Dali, he was dripping over his own edges. Without Sam, there was no one to anchor him, nothing to root him to a city filled with ghostly memories. He needed something primal, with presence and permanence, and the ancient peaks of the Blue Ridge called to him. There he hoped to find himself again. Or maybe for the first time.

The clock on the night table glowed 12:47. Julian turned on the lamp. Next to it he kept a photograph of him and Sam in a matte black frame. Their heads were slanted toward each other. They were smiling. They were happy. Julian picked up the photo and held it to his chest. It had been taken a few hours before his first gallery show. An abstract canvas hovered in the background, glaring, all edges and angles, defined geometry. Julian now thought the painting "untrue." He remembered the control with which he'd executed the placement of each line, each stroke, remembered how he'd squelched the blurry-edged swirl of emotion that spiraled within him, threatening to explode. It frightened him. If he gave it free rein, his work might appear capricious, artistically undisciplined. What would Sam have thought?

Julian traced Sam's image through the glass. To the eye it was flat and motionless, a frozen slice of ordinary late afternoon, a unique but unspectacular moment pressed in two dimensions. But looked at through the heart, it was round and warm and moving, a reflection Julian could fall into, a cloud of living memory floating him back to a time before death had dared to show its face. He pressed his lips to the vibrant, beautiful Sam who had once been. "I love you forever," he said.

Carefully setting the photo down, Julian slipped out of bed. He felt his way along the dark hallway into the kitchen to put on the tea kettle. Recessed overhead lighting lent a soft glow to the white refrigerator and range and the oak cabinets with their white porcelain knobs. When the kettle whistled, Julian fixed himself a cup of tea. He leaned against the pantry sipping, remembering—how Sam had coaxed him into midnight outings in search of cappuccino ice cream on a chocolate waffle cone, the endearing notes he'd left for Julian taped to the bathroom mirror, the way Sam's cheeks flushed when he'd fluffed the punch line to a joke.

Suddenly a voice interrupted. *It's time*, it whispered. Julian could have sworn it was Sam. He often talked to Sam to ease the loneliness on sleepless nights, but Sam had never talked back. *It's time.* The words echoed in Julian's mind. Sound floated back to him from every corner. *It's time...time...time.*

Trembling, Julian sensed a creative urgency overtake him. Something larger than himself directed him to the laundry room where he'd stored a stack of unpacked boxes. A painting was straining for life. That's what was happening. He hardly remembered what it felt like. Everything, he thought, had died with Sam, and not painting became Julian's self-inflicted punishment for still drawing breath. Besides, he'd felt sure his work had been marked by nothing more than triviality, that it made a mockery of art. Eventually, the Muses gave up trying to cajole him out of endless mourning. Inspiration dried to dust. Now, despite himself, he was slipping through the season of endings. A spring of imagination was stirring, welling from its center, luring him with its prism of possibility.

Barefooted, wearing only briefs, numb to the chill of midnight, Julian ripped packing tape off several cartons marked "art materials" and fished in the crumpled newsprint with his hands. Locating what he was looking for, he lifted two boxes and followed the unfamiliar path to his easel propped in a corner of the spare bedroom. His last stretched canvas leaned beside it. From one carton he chose several tubes and squeezed large ribbons of acrylic onto a palette—sienna, crimson, ebony, ash. With broad strokes, he began sweeping pigment across the canvas. He moved free and wild, an urgent, uncensored inspiration resounding, as if some part of him knew where he was heading.

*Life,* the voice said, louder this time, more insistent. As if in a trance, Julian added to his pallet cerulean, emerald, violet, fuchsia, gamboge—colors of sky and sea and summer meadow, of wildflowers and sunrise. Then, craving more than earthly hues, he searched for opalescent pearl, metallic silver.

By the time he put down his brushes, the first light of day had pierced a thin layer of cloud. Julian stepped back to see what had birthed itself. Before him was a visionary symphony— rich, textured patterns receding, swelling; shimmering, iridescent overlays that seemed to take on more dimension than the medium could allow. Impressions of an ideal, they suggested an atmosphere where reality was not about the well-defined detail and diminishing perspective of the eye, but about the nebulous and infinite landscapes of the heart.

Julian had never worked like that before. He'd never been so unaware of what translated itself onto his canvas. It was as if it had not been his own hand that painted. At least not the overcautious, self-critical one he was used to. What he saw before him was filled with vitality and promise. Sam would have approved, he was sure. "*Now* you're on to something, Jul," he would have said.

Exhilarated, Julian felt he'd opened his eyes after a long dark sleep. His body, down to its molecules, seemed rearranged and unsteady in its newness. Shivering, Julian searched in the closet for a blanket, found one and draped it around his shoulders. He lowered himself onto the rug. With more than his eyes, he navigated the artistic universe before him riding a wave, a spiral, a cluster, ravenous for what might be revealed at every turn. For the first time since Sam's death, Julian breathed freely, and tears flowed from the unexpected lightness of it.

# BLAME IT ON MERCURY

Finding a mouse in my car was the first sign my life was at the effect of planetary inversion. There I was matching wits with the furry three-inch menace, pleading with it to come out from under the seat, threatening to feed it to my cat Sasha. It was July hot and I was irritable and sweaty. But the mouse seemed cool as Camembert, watching me make a fool of myself. Then, it disappeared for good and I wasn't about to search it out. I had more important things to do. It was Sunday, and Jeremy, my lover, was coming over for dinner to celebrate our six-month anniversary

I'd met Jeremy at Happy Hair, the salon where I work as a stylist. We'd been drawn to each other from the minute he sat down in my chair. Even though I sensed imminent complication

— he being thirty-one to my nearly forty-two—we became involved almost immediately. Jeremy made me feel tingly in ways I'd forgotten since my ex-husband ran off with 1992's Miss Nude World.

Jeremy arrived at seven. I'd prepared salad and vegetarian lasagna (Jeremy hadn't eaten anything with hooves, wings or gills since he was ten). I'd meant to tell him about the mouse, but watching how he savored his food, closed his eyes every now and then, made soft "mmm" sounds as he chewed, moved my mind in a completely different direction. Soon, we were making love, perfect as ever, and afterwards, Jeremy lay with his head on my chest, his dark blonde hair in disarray across my breasts. As I stroked the soft stubble of his cheek, he began running his index finger in circles against my thigh, a familiar sign something was on his mind.

"Is anything the matter?" I said.

A long pause, then, "How do you know if you're gay?"

Without meaning to, I chuckled. "Gay as in homosexual?"

"Gay."

"If you have to ask," I said, "you're not."

I couldn't fathom that this sweetheart of a man, whom I, against my better judgment, had fallen in love with, was serious.

"Or bi," he said, his finger circles speeding up.

"Bi-sexual?"

"Yeah."

I stopped caressing his face and hair. "And what, pray tell, brought this on?"

"I don't know."

"You don't know! Are you telling me that during all these months we've been seeing each other, and after the way we just made love, you haven't been attracted to me?"

I sat up forcing Jeremy to roll off me. Suddenly feeling self-conscious in my female nakedness, I reached for the sheet and pulled it to my chin.

"No. No," Jeremy said, arranging himself against the pillows.

"No what? No you haven't been attracted to me? Or no, of course you have?" I searched his eyes.

"I have. I couldn't have pretended what's between us, Leah. You know I love you."

"Then what are we talking about here?"

"Promise you won't laugh."

"Okay," I lied. I wasn't making any promises.

"I told you I have an identical twin brother in Baltimore, right?"

"Right."

"Well, he called a few days ago and told me he was gay."

"You had no idea?"

"No. Well...maybe. I don't know." Jeremy lowered his eyes. "It just wasn't something we discussed." He fumbled with the sheets. "Anyway, my brother started talking about this boy Carlton who we both knew when we were twelve, and as I listened, I began to remember—or maybe imagined I remembered—the same kind of feelings he was describing. Sexual feelings."

"What happened when you were twelve?"

25

"Nothing. I guess the feelings sort of went away. For me at least. But not for Joshua."

"Are you attracted to men now?" I was afraid to hear the answer.

"I don't think so."

"What do you mean, you don't *think* so?" I jerked the covers over to my side of the bed exposing some of Jeremy's best parts.

"I don't know!"

There were lots of things Jeremy seemed not to know. He ran his fingers hard through his hair. He folded his arms across his chest, which made his beautiful shoulders look like sculpture. If we hadn't been having that inane conversation, I would have jumped his gorgeous bones again.

"I'm a little freaked, okay?" he said. "I think we should stop seeing each other for a while."

"What?" I turned so I could see his whole face.

With impeccably bad timing, Sasha, my cat, jumped onto Jeremy's side of the bed and anchored against his thigh. He seemed glad for the distraction. He smiled at her. Raising his voice several octaves the way people do when they talk to animals, he cooed at her, stroked her into a grinding purr. They were a mutual admiration society.

Jeremy turned back toward me as if I were an aside. "Just for a little while," he said, "so I can sort things out."

I'd heard that speech before.

"Exactly how are you going to 'sort things out'?"

"I don't know," he said.

Sasha meowed loudly.

"Is there anything you *do* know?"

"I need to go see Josh and talk to him. He told me he's been in therapy for the last three years. Maybe he knows something."

"If that's what you want. But I'm going to have to sort things out, too. And I don't know how I'll feel when I get all my curling irons in a row."

Jeremy looked at me with his pale blue eyes, now luminous with tears. I felt motherly. I hated feeling motherly. Moving closer to him, I took his hand. "It's okay, sweetie. Do what you have to do," I said, "but just for the record, I don't think you're gay."

Jeremy left for Baltimore on Monday morning. He told me he probably wouldn't call, that I shouldn't worry. "I promise I'll call the minute I get back," he said.

I didn't trust him. A man's promise is like a balloon. It floats for a while, but being mostly thin skin around a lot of hot air, it eventually explodes and fizzles.

I was off from work that day and tried to keep my mind occupied by making the weekly To Do lists Jeremy teased me about. By afternoon, however, I began contemplating the worst. What if he *was* gay and his brother introduced him to a young sexy man he fell passionately in love with? What if he wasn't gay and his brother introduced him to a young sexy *woman* he fell passionately in love with? Or...what if he became totally confused and frightened, shaved his head and cloistered himself in a monastery?

I puttered around the house attempting to shake such thoughts when it occurred to me that Sasha hadn't made an appearance in hours. I looked for her everywhere and finally found her deep inside the hole she'd torn in the box spring cover. Very attached to Jeremy, she probably sensed my agitation over an impending breakup and had already copped an attitude over his leaving. When I finally coaxed her out from under the bed, she darted into the living room. I rushed after her, trying to get hold of her. She loped across the coffee table, the couch, sprung onto a high oak bookcase and precariously perched on top. Then I noticed she was losing hair left and right. Gobs of it floated through the air, stuck to upholstery, nested in corners. The rest Sasha regurgitated all over my signed copy of *The Bridges of Madison County*.

By Tuesday morning, I seriously considered taking a few days off work to suck on Xanax and burrow under the covers, but when you're a hair stylist, missing work becomes a complicated matter. Clients don't wait for you like a pile of papers on a desk. They have to be called. They're not gracious about re-scheduling. They have roots overdue for color. They have bangs they've self-mutilated with kitchen shears. They have social events for which they *have* to have a cut and style. What they don't have is sympathy.

As I drove to the shop early, torturing over whether or not

I'd ever again feel Jeremy's lips along that shivery place on the back of my neck, I smelled something nauseating coming through the car's air vent. I had time before my first appointment and swung by Lester's Foreign Fix-It to see Sonny, my mechanic.

"Dead animal," he said. "Maybe snake."

I told him about the critter I'd chased after days before.

"Then definitely mouse," he said.

He surmised it had gotten into the engine and fried itself. He said it could be anywhere, in any of the cylinders or hoses. He told me he would have to take the entire engine apart (which would cost more than a trip to Bora Bora) and there was no guarantee he would ever find it.

"Sell the car," he said. "Or live with it. It'll go away. Eventually." He paused, then sniffed around the back seat. "What's that other smell?"

"What other smell?

"Like one of them light-in-the-loafers guys you work with spilled some fancy after shave."

It was Jeremy's cologne that Sonny had gotten a whiff of. It had leaked out of his overnight bag the week before. I hadn't noticed it for days. I wondered if there were other things connected with Jeremy I hadn't noticed. I felt ill.

It was the middle of summer and I couldn't use the A/C or fresh air vents. The smell was so bad, I had to leave the windows wide open. I bought pine-scented air fresheners to hang from the door handles, patchouli incense to burn in the ashtray, and, for extra measure, I sprinkled potpourri on the carpet.

When I got to Happy Hair, I looked like hell. The puffs beneath my red-veined eyes made them appear sunken. Auburn frizz corkscrewed defiantly from my shoulder-length tresses. Louis, stylist and drama queen, entered with a familiar flourish signaling no good and I wasn't in the mood.

"Ooohhhhh, that man is plaguing my sanity," he whined with a thick southern drawl.

"What now?" I said.

"He's breakin' my heart, lyin' all the time, telling me he'll call when he won't, cheating on me with that twenty-two year old brassyblonde queen from Tennessee."

It was another episode of *Latino Lust*, and I didn't have the patience. "Maybe it's time to call it quits with Paolo. Take care of yourself for a change." I knew I sounded a bit cold-hearted.

"Well, you don't have to get uppity with me, Lee-ahh." Louis set his bag down at the booth next to mine. He sank into his hip, eyed the slightly rounded figure in the mirror and fluffed up his spiky highlighted hair. He adjusted his glasses, then tied on his apron.

"I'm sorry," I said. "I'm having troubles of my own."

"Like what?"

"Just because I don't air my personal drama in front of everyone doesn't mean I don't have a life," I said. "There's a dead mouse frying itself in the engine of my car and my…"

Louis interrupted. "Eeeeww. Mice give me the eebee geebies."

He sounded like a wuss. I wondered if Jeremy would have reacted the same way. "My cat Sasha is going bald," I continued.

"And Jeremy and I are separated."

"What happened with Jeremy?"

"He thinks he's gay."

A lascivious grin stretched across Louis's face. "Honey, that's the best news I've heard in forever! I knew it. I just knew it. That boy is hot!"

Did everyone know except me? "Thanks a lot, Louis." I was close to a meltdown.

"Just joking," Louis said, then seemed to rethink the statement. "Sort of."

Desperate to change the subject, I turned toward the mirror and tried to rearrange my unruly curls. "Look at this mess. I look like *The Bride of Frankenstein*."

Louis sized up my hair situation. "It's times like these a little product can work wonders." He paused. "Well, on second thought, maybe not in this case."

"You're a real riot this morning."

"Actually your hair looks great," he said. "Very sexy."

I felt about as sexy as a lug nut. A renegade tear rolled down my cheek.

For a moment, Louis actually seemed concerned. "Are you all right?"

"No." I grabbed a tissue.

"Mercury's still retrograde, you know," Louis said.

"Meaning?"

"Meaning, astrologically, it's going backwards. That could be why your life feels like watching *General Hospital* on bad acid. About the cat, I know this animal psychic you could call."

"Animal psychic, huh."

"I'm serious, Leah. She's really good. One time Mama's Shih Tzu, Babycakes, got into some used chewing gum and Mama tried to cut it out with pinking shears. Anyway, the dog was traumatized, wouldn't go potty in public for days. She had to have an indoor litter box. But Esmeralda, that's the psychic, straightened her out. Let me give you her number."

"Fine," I said. It was easier than debating the issue.

All day, I couldn't stop thinking of Jeremy and how I could have let myself get involved with him. I knew better. I swore I'd learned my lesson with Kevin and would never again fall for a younger man. Kevin who came on full of charm, oozing testosterone, trying to impress me with how sensitive he was, how he preferred a more mature woman in the prime of her beauty and sensuality. Then, just as I began to believe him, he disappeared without so much as a nod, as if he'd never witnessed my dreams or whispered longingly in the night. Without explanation, he left his shirt in my closet and his hook in my heart, and I found myself feeling old and ugly and very foolish.

Yet, in the light of Jeremy's smile, even the worst humiliation had receded into shadow. It took me five seconds to know I wasn't going to turn away from him. Jeremy was young, but he was wise and funny and caring and very sexy. He wasn't afraid to talk about things that mattered either, or to express his feelings. He listened to me when I needed a sympathetic ear, often showed me that the most intimate communication was beyond words, in a look, a touch, a smile. And to him, our age difference seemed unimportant. *I* was the one who continued to bring it up, not Jeremy. Once, he caught me in front of the mirror stretching my drooping skin toward my temples, trying to smooth out the years.

"Your face is lovely just the way it is," he said. "But what drew me to you most was your heart."

"It isn't fair," I said. I was still thinking about the betrayal of the body.

"It's your hang up, *chérie,* not mine." He slid his arms around me and kissed me on the cheek. "And I suggest you get over it, cause I plan to be around for a long while."

But when you've just turned forty-two, uncertainties surface with each new wrinkle and you feel you're headed straight downhill. I don't mean easy coasting either, but the quick descent into inevitable undesirability. Jeremy was thirty-one. As much as he professed not to care, it was only a matter of time before he no longer found me attractive.

*I think we should stop seeing each other.* His recent words reverberated. They were a far cry from *I plan to be around for a long while.* Up until our ridiculous conversation Sunday night, I thought we were doing better than I could ever have hoped. Now I wondered if I had once again cast my pearls before someone who had mistaken them for worthless paste.

On Wednesday, I somehow managed to make it through a full schedule at the salon. But later, at home, I flipped on the TV and found myself in the middle of *Saturday Night Fever,* an old favorite film of mine. Less than two weeks before, I'd gotten a reluctant Jeremy to watch the video with me, teased him mercilessly about how macho John Travolta was in his younger days, how he could really turn a woman on. I remembered how Jeremy hadn't wanted to make love afterwards. Now, smashing the off button on the remote, I dissolved into a twelve-tissue pity party.

When I recovered, I noticed, for the third day, Sasha had hardly eaten a thing. She also wouldn't cuddle with me on the couch or rub against my legs. She drank water out of the toilet bowl and peed in my Philodendron. She scratched and licked, hair flying like milkweed, mangy patches behind her ears, her back end looking like a feline Chihuahua. I began to take it very personally—first Jeremy, then my own cat rejecting me. At my wit's end, I called Louis's animal psychic, Esmeralda.

"I can do it over the phone," she said, "but I prefer to meet with Sasha in person. It just happens I had a cancellation. I could come over tonight."

Esmeralda arrived an hour later. Hardly the airy fairy I'd expected, she was a short, box-shaped woman probably in her late fifties. She wore too much make-up, was dressed in polyester, and her poofy hair was self-dyed a very pink strawberry blonde. Over her shoulder she carried a bulging blue canvas bag.

"I need to create the proper atmosphere," she said. "Do you mind if I move a few things around?"

Before I could reply, she began adjusting couch pillows, turning down lights, moving chairs. She took out an assortment of crystals—purple, bronze, clear. She lit a lavender-colored votive candle and placed it in a glass holder she'd brought with her.

"What exactly are you going to do?" I said.

"Ssshhhh. We must be very quiet."

She took out an abalone shell, a lighter, a small jar of white, stiff-looking leaves.

"Sage," she said.

She lit the sage then blew out the fire, leaving smoking embers. I coughed. Esmeralda swirled the smoke around. The hairs left on Sasha's body rose like porcupine quills. Visually stalking Esmeralda as if she had tiny ears and a tasty tail, Sasha bared her teeth. Her kitty eyes became bloodshot. She sneezed.

"We have to clear the vibrations," Esmeralda said.

"Of course." I slumped onto the couch.

After numerous mumbled incantations, Esmeralda announced she was ready to contact Sasha's Inner Transcendent Catness. She sat down in an arm chair and closed her eyes. "Good," she whispered. "Yes. I understand." She took a breath. "Sasha tells me you're not cleaning her litter box often enough, and you've changed her brand of food."

The furry little traitor. "She *told* you that?"

"Yes."

"Well, just what kind of food would she like?"

"She says she wants the gourmet kind. With the exotic names. In the little cans."

This was Jeremy's doing. He'd spoiled her with those little gourmet cans. "She said 'exotic names'?"

"There *is* a certain amount of translation involved," Esmeralda explained.

"I see."

Esmeralda continued. "She tells me she's irritated, that she's been scratching to get your attention, that she feels traumatized by your suppressed hostility."

Sasha hissed at me. I hissed back.

"She's trying to tell me about a man."

"She must mean Jeremy, my...boyfriend."

"Has he left?"

"He's in Baltimore." I didn't owe her any explanations.

"Well, Sasha seems to feel he's not coming back. And that it's your fault."

"Oh she does, does she?" I was ready to get out my clippers and buzz the rest of that cat bald.

"Do I detect a little hostility?" Esmeralda said.

*You're the psychic. Read my mind.*

Esmeralda turned to Sasha. "You poor thing. I *do* understand."

I was very close to throwing her and her psychic self out.

"Sasha thinks you've been jealous of how close she and this Jeremy have become. She says just because he prefers feline females to human ones is no reason to chase him away. She says you always chase away the ones she likes."

My own Sasha, who I raised from an orphaned kitten, had turned against me.

"Sasha says Jeremy was different from those sweaty guys, that he always smelled good."

36

Could I possibly have missed something? First Sonny, then Louis, now even my cat thinks Jeremy is gay.

"Do I get to have anything translated from me back to her," I said, "or is this a one-sided conversation?"

"Sasha doesn't want to talk anymore." Esmeralda blinked a few times, quickly got up, blew out the candle, packed her paraphernalia, and announced there wasn't much else she could do. "If I were you," she said, "I would see a good therapist."

I paid her reluctantly and showed her to the door. Sasha sauntered out of the room wagging her hairless butt at me as if to say, "So there." Suppressed hostility indeed! There was nothing suppressed about my hostility. It was clearly aimed at Her Regal Feline Highness.

Exhausted and agitated, I headed for the bedroom. I was pathetic. And I was tired of being pathetic. What was I doing letting a bald-butted, four-legged vamp with an attitude humiliate me? I went over to the bed, where I knew Sasha was hiding in the box spring, and flopped down hard. She meowed.

"*I'm* in charge here," I shouted, "and I'm through with this nonsense. Yours and Jeremy's and the whole cosmic retro conspiracy."

I'd spun myself out of orbit and I was ready to reclaim my own little corner of the universe. One week ago, I would have sworn there was no way Jeremy could be gay. Now I wasn't so sure, and much to my surprise, I no longer cared one way or the other. I undressed down to my bikini underwear and slipped into a tank top. Suddenly, even at forty-two, I felt pretty darn sexy. If Jeremy was gay, it was his loss. The last few days it had seemed as if all the planets, especially Venus, were heading backwards. Like I'd somehow taken a detour into the dark side of Oz. I crawled my tired self into bed, put on my mental ruby slippers, clicked the heels three times, declared out loud, "I'd just better wake up back in Kansas" and fell into a deep sleep.

The next morning I felt more rested than I had all week, so when Jeremy returned earlier than I'd expected and called that evening, I was ready. He asked if he could come over. I told him he could. I didn't bring up the subject of his time away, and he didn't offer anything. Despite my recent burst of self-confidence, or maybe because of it, the sound of his voice reminded me how much I still cared.

As Jeremy's car pulled up, I waited to hear his key in the lock. He knocked instead. Not a good sign. My stomach did a little jitterbug. Preparing myself for the worst, I opened the door. He stood outside the threshold, obviously struggling to hold a straight face. I stared at him for a long time.

"I didn't want to leave any doubt," he said.

There he was in black boots, ivory bell-bottom slacks that revealed more than they concealed, a black polyester shirt circa 1977, sleeves rolled twice, buttons opened almost to the waist, gold chains draped around his neck. Losing his grip on composure, his mouth widened into a smirk. Rhythmically, he thrust his pelvis to a silent beat. There was no doubt. He had all the right moves. John Travolta had never looked so good.

I motioned Jeremy through the door and into the living

room. He handed me a dark chocolate truffle bar, my favorite. "Sweets for my sweetie," he said. He kissed me. "And this is for Sasha."

Upon hearing her name, Sasha dashed across the living room floor, skidded to a stop and rubbed back and forth against Jeremy's pant leg. That's when he noticed. "What happened to her hair!"

"It's a long story," I said. "I'll tell you later."

No way was I going to let that cat spoil this reunion.

"I brought you something, too," Jeremy said to Sasha, scratching under her chin. He handed me a small, sealed package. "Look what I found at a gourmet pet shop."

I read the label: Flash-Fried Mouse Treats.

I smiled. Then grinned. Then burst into laugh-out-loud relief. Perhaps Mercury was finally heading in the right direction, because at that moment, everything felt blissfully on course.

# Why Stefan Had To Rent A Sander And Refinish The Floors In Brenda's Bedroom

When the cashier prematurely and automatically, without a twinge of uncertainty, gave her a senior discount, Brenda felt compelled to paint every room in her house Chinese red. She went to Lowe's and sorted through palette samples. Chinese red turned out not to be so simple. She compared tints and hues, finally deciding on a shade that reminded her of a clingy swingy dress she'd worn to see Baryshnikov dance Romeo at Lincoln Center decades ago when her hair had pigment and her skin knew how to hold itself in place.

Not having painted anything in a while, Brenda asked the twelve year old "design consultant" named Binky what else she would need. He helped her gather painter's tape, stir sticks, rollers, brushes, plastic, all of which she carted home along with eight gallons of Peking Passion. She wondered what Stefan would think. They'd only been lovers for two months and were still at the stage of undressing by candlelight, and watching each other sleep. He had not yet witnessed female hormones—or the lack thereof—run amok.

Brenda began with her bedroom. She flipped on Ravel's *Bolero*, shoved furniture, draped, taped, then rolled overlapping v's along the wall behind the bed, burying forever all traces of Perfect Pearl. Feeling the echo of horns and drums rumble in her belly, she dipped a brush, wrote WILD WOMAN in letters two-feet high on the adjacent wall. Heavy spatters of crimson sprayed her cheeks. Her hair became an impressionistic blob spreading across her old Kirov Ballet t-shirt. The music opened, wound back on itself, ascended. She dipped again, wrote HOT TOMALE, added HOOCHIE MAMA ROJA. She grabbed the old paint-speckled towel from the corner, slid it around her blue-jeaned hips, swished it from side to side. Cajoled by a swell of strings climbing toward crescendo, her body searched for a *developpé*, an *arabesque*, an *entrechat-six* it could not find. *Bolero* thrashed and pounded to climax. Brenda, trembling, collapsed to the floor. So much red was unsettling, like playing with more fire than she remembered how to handle.

# Harry Meets The Goddess

Harry Gold stood in line at the supermarket imagining how he would compose his letter to *Penthouse.* The object of his lust was at the checkout one aisle over. She couldn't have been more than twenty-five, with the required 36C breasts, blond hair to her waist, and jeans tight enough to reveal she wasn't wearing any underwear. Harry was up to *then she ran her big blue eyes slowly down my body, and seductively said, "I wonder if you'd mind helping me carry these groceries to my car..."* when the cashier broke his trance.

"Sir. Sir? That'll be $47.58."

"Oh," Harry said. He pulled his wallet from his pocket. When he looked again, the young woman was gone.

Women were always disappearing on Harry, the last being

his wife, Shari, who had asked him for a divorce the year before.

"You're a pig, Harry," she'd said. "I'm leaving you." Shari was not one for beating around the bush.

"What!" Harry shouted. "What did I do?" He'd given her a nice house on Long Island, expensive jewelry, a new car every other year.

"If you try real hard," Shari said, "I'm sure you'll figure it out."

But Harry hadn't figured it out. Not all of it, anyway. Harry was from Brooklyn. And this, according to Shari, was why there were a lot of things he hadn't figured out.

Harry had a medium build with a few middle-aged pounds settled into what he called "love handles." His coarse, still mostly dark hair sprung short and Brillo-y around his head. His skin was olive, his eyes the color of weak coffee, and he had an aquiline nose with a slight bump near the top. But his most remarkable feature was a dimple deep in his left cheek which, when he smiled, made people expect something more congenial than what usually came out of his mouth.

The last time Harry was single, the passwords to pleasure were straightforward, contained no subtleties, no subtexts. "Your place or mine? or "Do you wanna do it?"—short and to the point, just like the act—had pretty much gotten him what he wanted.

Now, at fifty-one, Harry felt cheated by a world where women did not operate the way they used to. Now, he encountered a whole new breed who wanted not just to climb into a man's bed, but to penetrate his soul. Women who seemed to breathe a lot and use words like tantra and spiritual union. Worse yet, women who worshipped Oprah, the person who, according to Harry, was single-handedly responsible for the whole unfortunate evolution of the female sex. Things have gotten far too complicated, he thought as he gathered his groceries.

Harry deposited the bags in the trunk of his Olds Cutless Supreme and slid behind the wheel. He was about to turn the key in the ignition when his eyes were drawn toward the seat beside him. A woman was sitting there, a woman he would swear on his father's grave had not been next to him a millisecond before.

"Who the hell are you?" he asked, in his usual gallant manner.

"The goddess," she replied, focused on fastening her seatbelt. "Well, one of them at any rate."

"The WHAT?"

"The godddessss," she repeated, slowly this time, looking him right in the eyes so it might sink in. "But you can call me Lu."

"Lu." Harry stared in disbelief.

"It's short for Luna, which is so affected, don't you think?"

Harry wasn't paying attention. A goddess named Lu, he thought. Perhaps this was some kind of hallucination caused by too many lascivious fantasies. Perhaps he was even more desperate than he realized, for in Harry's humble opinion, Lu was not exactly goddess material.

The woman sitting beside him was in the prime of her

forties, yet she radiated an ageless quality which Harry totally missed. Her shoulder-length auburn hair was gathered loosely at the nape of the neck, the shorter lengths at the top and sides falling in soft waves and wispy tendrils around her cheeks and forehead. Her eyes were hazel brown with generous lids, her face heart-shaped. Except for a natural blush, her skin was very fair. And in her ears she wore tiny iridescent pearl earrings.

What Harry saw, however, was a pale, middle-aged lady at least ten pounds overweight with no boobs. Still, the situation would have been less than suspicious, except for the fact that it was November and this woman was wearing a sleeveless, semi-transparent, calf-length tunic, and seemingly nothing else.

"This is some kind of joke, right?" Harry prayed it was true. It must be Bernie's idea, he thought. Only his friend Bernie, who constantly teased him about his non-existent sex life, could have such a warped sense of humor. "Bernie put you up to this, didn't he?"

"Who?" Lu hugged herself, shivering. "Do you have a blanket or something? I always have a little trouble pinpointing which season I'm going to wind up dropping into."

Harry was about to lose it. "Okay, this has gone far enough. You can get out of the car right now."

"Oh no," Lu said with sudden seriousness. "You don't understand. I can't leave you. I was 'sent.'"

"Sent?"

"Yes, 'sent.'"

"Riiight." Harry thought perhaps Lu was a few cards shy of a full deck. "I'll just drive you home, okay?" he said as if

45

speaking to a child. "Where do you live?"

"For now, I guess I live wherever you do." Lu's teeth began to chatter. "Do you think you could at least turn on some heat?"

Keeping his eyes on Lu, Harry tried to blink her away. When she didn't disappear, he turned on the ignition and pushed the heat lever to high. "It should warm up in a minute or two," he said. He wondered why he was talking to this person as if she were a rational human being.

Harry didn't know what to do next, but Lu seemed to.

"We should go home now, Harry," she said. "There's really nothing else you can do. Trust me. Once I've been 'sent' I have to stay with you until I complete the assignment. Besides, you have perishables in the trunk."

"I'm an 'assignment'?"

"Yes you are, Harry. And a tough one so far."

Maybe there was something going on here Harry had missed. "Am I dead?"

"Of course not. You're as alive as I am."

"Oh that's *really* comforting."

"If you were dead, you'd be a lot smarter."

Harry thought he was smart enough. He may not have finished Queens College, but he hadn't done so bad. He had a nice house, which he got to keep since Shari moved back to The Bronx. He'd made Salesman of the Month three times in a row after sliding a whole lot of customers behind the wheel of a shiny new Oldsmobile. And he hadn't even gotten caught that one time, two years before, when he'd returned a kiss thrust upon him, tongue and all, by Doreen, the horny widow down the street. Well, at least not until months later when she got annoyed with him and opened her big mouth to Shari.

And now, even though he'd been a man who usually kept out of "women's work," he'd actually learned to sort his laundry before washing it so the whites didn't become pink or gray, and to clean the hair from the bathroom sink after shaving. He'd even invented his very own recipe for bourbon chili. He lived pretty well, he thought, despite those damned alimony payments which, mind you, he always made on time. How much smarter could he be dead?

It became obvious Lu wasn't going away, so Harry eased out of the parking lot. The sun, low in the autumn sky, streaked through the front windshield casting seductive shadows over Lu's anatomy. Suddenly, she didn't look half bad and Harry thought maybe he needed to reassess the situation. After all, Lu *was* female. She appeared to have all the right body parts. And little boobs were better than no boobs at all. Besides, maybe after he'd made her moan his name, she'd be willing to do womanly things for him like cook a decent meal and straighten up around the house, things Harry really missed since Shari had left.

*Dear Penthouse, you will never believe my story, but here goes. This woman who says she is "the goddess" appears in my car one day. She's about twenty-five with blond hair to her waist and firm 36C breasts that are straining to be squeezed. I can tell all this because she's only wearing a see-through toga, like something out of the orgy scene in Caligula. When I ask her where she came from, she says she's been "sent" just for me. She keeps looking at me with her sultry blue eyes. She licks her lips, and I can see her squeeze her thighs together just enough for me to notice. Well as you can imagine, I'm having to do all I can to keep from jumping her bones right there in the car. "Let's go back to your place," she says. "That's just fine by me," I say, and start to drive us home. Meanwhile, I'm trying to figure out what I might have done to deserve a goddess, but it turns out to be too much for my brain to handle. All I want is to stick my tongue down her throat, take a few licks at those tits and ride her like there's no tomorrow...*

"Not a chance," the real Lu said.

"What?" Harry replied, startled.

"There are no secrets, Harry. And you have a very limited idea of what a sexy woman is."

"Holy shit! You can read my mind?"

"Afraid so."

Harry began to panic. Since his divorce, his mind had become triple X-rated. He would say it was because he'd been married for so long and hadn't had any really exciting sex for decades. But the truth was thinking raunchy thoughts distracted him from feeling how much he missed Shari, even her yelling, even her restless poking arms in the night. And how guilty he felt. Sometimes Harry thought he and Shari were like a bad TV sitcom that managed to stay on year after year—she nagging at him, he talking big, acting wimpy. He could have been a more loving husband. He knew that. That's why he didn't fight too hard when Shari had said she wanted out. Not that she was perfect, far from it, but Harry felt maybe Shari had deserved better.

Harry looked at Lu. I've got to stop thinking, Harry thought. Especially about sex. But how can I stop thinking about sex with a half-naked woman sitting next to me?  Shit! I can't think that either. Okay, I'll think about nothing. I'll hum. Harry began to hum a random melody.

 Lu turned to him with an *it won't work* expression on her face.

"Shit!  This is ridiculous," he muttered. *I want you to go away.* He aimed the thought at Lu like a laser. *I want you to go away right now! Go away!*

"It's no use, Harry."

"Isn't there some kind of law against eavesdropping in someone's mind?"

Lu didn't answer.

Screw her, Harry thought. I'll think whatever the hell I want to. So what if she knows. What's she going to do, wash my mind out with soap? Report me to the porno police?  First she'd have to explain her half-naked self, now, wouldn't she? Read my mind if you want. See if I care. Harry glanced over at Lu as if daring her.

"If it makes you feel any better Harry, I can only do it when I want to, if I focus on doing it. And since your thoughts aren't all that interesting, I'd just as soon stay out of them."

"That suits me fine."

Harry turned left onto Cedar, then right onto Sycamore Road where he lived. Thank God he had a garage. At least he wouldn't have to explain Lu and her toga to his nosy neighbors.

He activated the garage door opener and pulled in. He remembered his house was its usual mess, and wondered if he would lose some kind of cosmic brownie points for it. But then he figured, if Lu didn't like it, she could either disappear the way she came or clean it up, the first option now being his personal preference.

Lu, however, opted for the second and immediately began to create order out of the chaos in his living room.

"Don't get used to this, Harry," she said as she disposed of empty Michelob bottles and weeks worth of Newsday. "It's just my nature to do what's in front of me. It's a Zen thing."

For the next forty-five minutes, Lu washed dishes, wiped countertops, vacuumed taco and potato chip crumbs from the carpet, Windexed the glass-top coffee and end tables, turned and fluffed couch cushions. "How can you live in such disarray?"

"Very easily," Harry said. Lu's words reminded him too much of Shari's, although Shari would have said them much louder. And she would have said, "A PIG STY. HOW CAN YOU LIVE IN SUCH A PIG STY?"

It was almost completely dark now, and Harry turned on another light. He watched Lu as she scurried around, but didn't offer to help. He'd never been good at those things. The times he'd tried to clean the house, Shari said it wasn't worth it, that she'd only have to do it over. She told him he always missed spots when he dusted, and didn't vacuum all the dirt underneath the chairs. So Harry stuck to things he was good at, like selling cars and making smartass remarks.

In case Lu was tuned in, Harry tried not to think anything too self-deprecating. But he had to figure out what to do about this crazy woman taunting him with a see-through toga, taking over his life as if she was settling in for the long haul.

A minute later, the phone rang. It was Bernie. As much as he knew he'd regret it, and even though Lu was probably tuned into every word, Harry filled Bernie in on what had happened. He needed to tell someone.

"I don't believe a word of it," Bernie said. "I'll be over in ten minutes to see for myself."

"You'll believe it soon enough."

When Harry went back to check on Lu, he hardly recognized his own house. The living room, dining room and kitchen looked like a photo out of *Good Housekeeping*. Lu was still there, standing at the stove, basting something that smelled exactly like Shari's pot roast, Harry's favorite. Over her tunic, she had on his bright blue muslin apron with the words BBQ King written in white across the front. The back of her, however, was still semi-transparent, and Harry couldn't help eyeing her ample and inviting behind. The whole scene, as absurd as it was, presented possibilities that made him hopeful. The doorbell interrupted his fantasy, and Harry heard Bernie let himself in through the unlocked door. He rushed to intercept him.

Harry had been friends with Bernie for five years, several spent working with him at the same car dealership. When they'd met, Bernie, himself divorced, was living with a woman named Isabel. Shari and Isabel shared complaining about their men and got on famously. A month after Shari left Harry, Isabel split from

Bernie, taking more than her share of their household furnishings with her, and after that, Bernie traded selling cars for selling electronic security systems. It was a continual mystery to Harry how Bernie could get a woman to share the same conversation with him, never mind the same bed. But somehow he could, and as a sideline, Bernie put himself in charge of checking up on Harry's sex life.

"Hey buddy," Bernie said, examining himself in the hall mirror. The five hairs left on the top of his head were standing at attention from the wind. He smoothed them down. He took out a six inch pocket comb, the kind last seen in the hands of Elvis Presley or James Dean, and ran it through the only slightly more abundant rest of his hair. He didn't bother to take off his orange and black ski jacket. "So where is this 'goddess'?"

"In the living room," Harry said. "Look for yourself."

Bernie walked into the living room while Harry waited in the hallway. Three seconds later, Bernie came out. "Have you lost your mind?  There's a woman in there, but she's no half-naked goddess."

"What do you mean?"

Harry bolted through the archway, part of him hoping Lu had finally taken off, another part hoping she hadn't so he wouldn't look like a total idiot. Lu was still there, sitting on the couch, but instead of her sheer toga, she was dressed in black wool slacks and a burgundy boat neck sweater, her legs tightly crossed. "

So you're Harry's goddess," Bernie said with a smirk. He walked toward her.

"I'm Lu."

"Hi 'Lu.'" He emphasized her name. "I'm Bernie."

"Nice to meet you."

"Be careful, Bernie, she can read your thoughts," Harry said.

Bernie sat down next to her. He stared at her sweater. Lu didn't flinch.

"Harry says you can read my thoughts."

Lu seemed amused. "So he does."

"Well, can you?"

"Can you read mine?"

Bernie moved away from her a bit. "If you ask me, you sound more like a shrink than a goddess."

"Interesting," Lu replied.

"Okay," Harry said. "Enough of this bullshit." He turned to Lu. "You're making me look like a fool. And a liar."

"I'm sorry Harry. I don't mean to."

Harry looked at Bernie. "I think you better leave, okay?"

"Sure, Harry." Bernie seemed to humor him. He got up and headed for the door.

"Bye 'Lu.'" He leaned in toward Harry's ear. "She's no goddess, buddy, but whatever she is, you ought to be grateful. Maybe you'll get lucky."

At that moment, Harry found Bernie's condescending remarks even more irritating than usual. "Get out of here," he said, following him to the door, locking it behind him.

He stormed back to the living room. "Just what the hell is going on?"

"Did you expect me to sit around in a toga and explain myself to your friend?" Lu said calmly. "I'm a goddess, Harry. I don't explain myself to anyone. Besides, I was 'sent' for you. My business is with you, not with Bernie or anyone else, and I'd appreciate it if you would please remember that." She did not sound unkind.

"I'm sorry, okay?"

"As long as we understand each other."

Harry wanted to ask Lu where she'd gotten the clothes and the food, how she knew the recipe for Shari's pot roast and how she cooked it so fast, but he thought it best to keep his mouth shut for a change. He guessed if she really was a goddess, she could do a lot of miraculous things, and as much as he tried not to, Harry couldn't help thinking about what miracles she might be able to work in the bedroom and whether or not he could get her to perform them on him.

Harry's first week with Lu was nothing like he'd expected. Lu slept in the guest room, wore normal clothing which she seemed to pull out of thin air, continued to cook some of his meals (other times they ordered take-out) and helped him around the house. They played gin rummy in the evenings, or watched TV. She never yelled. For a while, she hardly spoke at all.

"I'm making assessments," she'd say, sometimes indicating slight yes or no gestures with her head as if communicating with someone unseen.

Harry didn't know what to make of all that quiet. Most of his life he'd been surrounded by women—his mother, his aunts, his sister, his wife—who had not addressed him without raising their voices at least a thousand decibels. Sound bellowed around them like a force field that kept all men at distance. But with Lu, it was different. Something inviting hovered in her air. It filled his house. It felt peaceful, made him feel relaxed, like he didn't have to put on a show. When he came home each day, it welcomed him. He could slip into it like a favorite sweater, feel warm and safe inside of it. It made him want to remember to put the toilet seat down.

Harry thought about what he might have had with Shari if he hadn't been so self-centered, and had more often kept his own voice down a few decibels. He waited for Lu's "assessments," waited for her to rail against him for having been a lousy husband, a cosmic embarrassment to his sex. He wanted it, so he could get it over with. That was why she'd been sent, wasn't it? The goddess bit was only a tease, a cover-up. He waited for the wrath of God himself to be visited upon him for having been an over all despicable human being.

By the second week, Harry found himself inspired to do things he'd never done before. Maybe it was because Lu, unlike Shari, hadn't gotten on his case about anything. With Shari, there was always an objection—to the way he chewed his food, to the angle at which he draped the bathroom towels on the rack, to the sound he made when he sneezed with a very loud HAH-SHIT on the exhale. Now, Harry found himself saying "please" and "thank you." Twice, he complimented Lu on her outfits. One day, for no reason at all, Harry had the impulse to buy her flowers, and not just the cellophaned bunches you could get at the supermarket either. Harry drove out of his way to a real florist shop and had the woman (to whom he hardly gave his usual once over) make up a bouquet of peach colored roses he really liked, decorated with ferns and baby's breath. They cost a fortune.

When he gave them to Lu, he prepared himself for some hurtful remark like "you must have a guilty conscience over something, Harry," or "whatever it is you want from me Harry, flowers aren't going to do it." Instead, Lu took the bouquet and cradled it in her arms. She inhaled deeply of its subtle fragrance.

"They're just lovely, Harry," she said. "How thoughtful of you."

On Saturday, over their dinner of pepperoni pizza, Harry mustered the courage to try having a serious talk with Lu. There were things he had to get to the root of.

"Okay," he began, "I know why you're here."

"And why is that, Harry?"

"To punish me, right?" He picked off a piece of pepperoni and popped it in his mouth as if rewarding himself for finally having spoken up.

"Of course not. I am not here to berate or judge you, Harry. You do a very good job of that all by yourself." Lu took a sip of the Michelob she'd gotten in the habit of sharing with him. "Why haven't you ever asked who sent me?"

Harry didn't know why he hadn't asked. Maybe he'd been a little afraid of the answer. What if Lu had been sent by weird

Uncle Leo who claimed connections to the netherworld? Or worse, by Shari's recently dead Aunt Shirley who'd hurled matzo balls at him across the dinner table and on her deathbed threatened to cast an evil eye on him for eternity? But now Harry was ready. "Okay," he said. "I'm asking. Who sent you?"

"You did, Harry."

"I sent you?"

"Yes, Harry. You're the one who sent me."

On the surface, it sounded preposterous, yet down deep in his gut something rang true.

"You think this is about what's between your legs, Harry, but it's not. It's about what's in your heart."

Slowly, Lu reached out her hand and held the open palm an inch in front of the center of his chest. He could feel a warmth radiating from it. No one had ever before addressed Harry's heart. He felt this tremulous rumble rise from that deep down true place like a river when a dam breaks, and before he knew it, an unstoppable torrent poured down his cheeks. Harry hadn't cried since he was ten years old and his dog Ziggy had gotten hit by a car. He hadn't even cried when his father died, or when Shari had miscarried their baby, or when, after twenty-one years, she'd told him she wanted to end their marriage. He wondered if Lu had cast some kind of spell over him. Besides being able to read his mind, maybe she could control it as well.

Harry felt embarrassed. Grown men didn't cry. He buried his face in his hands. "What the hell are you doing to me?"

"You've needed this for a long time, Harry." Lu got up and brought him a box of tissues. For the first time, she touched him, stroked his hair. "It's all right, Harry." She pulled him against her, let him wrap his arms around her waist and weep into her breast. Under any other circumstance, Harry would have had his hands all over her, but at that moment it didn't even cross his mind.

"I feel like..." Harry began, but couldn't finish. A broken man, he thought.

"You're not," Lu said. "It takes courage to call the goddess to you. The larger You sent me here not to make you broken, but to break you open. There's a new Harry emerging, one who will no longer be addressed as swine. The old sitcom has finally been cancelled."

Harry reached for another tissue. There was nothing he could say to a woman who had seen him turn to total mush right before her. He could hardly look at her. He wasn't sure about this new Harry, but the old one thought it would be nice not to be called a pig.

"Harry," Lu said.

He could sense what was coming. *Don't go.*

"I have to Harry. The assignment is completed. I'm being called back."


Late that night, as Harry drifted between awake and asleep, Lu came into his room. He could see by the slatted moonlight through the partially opened blinds she was wearing the tunic she had arrived in.

"I couldn't leave without saying goodbye, Harry," she

whispered.

Whether or not he dreamed what followed, he would never know for sure. Without saying another word, Lu slipped under the covers and slid over next to him. He thought he had died and gone to heaven.

When Harry awoke the next morning he knew Lu was gone for good, yet the peacefulness she'd brought to him remained. It was Sunday and there was no hurry to get up. Harry pulled the covers to his chin and closed his eyes. He re-lived the night before.

*Dear Penthouse, in a million years I never could have imagined I'd be writing this. One day, not too long ago, a goddess named Luna showed up in my life. I don't mean goddess in the sense you think I do. This was a real goddess, and she had none of the things I'd always fantasized about. She was not blonde. She did not have 36C breasts. And she was probably almost twice twenty-five. Yet she made love to me as if I were a god. This didn't happen from the start. I had to wait weeks until she'd even let me touch her. But on that last night, before she had to return to wherever goddesses come from, she snuck into my room and slipped naked into my bed. "This is against the rules," she said, "but I just can't resist you." Then she...*

Harry tried to continue, to describe all the ways in which they'd made love and how many times, but found he couldn't. Suddenly, it did not feel right to tell anything to anyone. Not *Penthouse*. Not even Bernie. He lay back and watched the morning flicker through the room like polished gold. He stretched his naked limbs between the sheets, and for a moment, he thought he detected the comforting aroma of Shari's pot roast.

# POSSOONS

Susan sat naked in the middle of the bed, legs laced in a half-lotus. A heart drawn between her breasts in Perfect Plum lipstick marked the place where her real one now felt crushed. She pressed her hand to it, breathed in its meaning. She felt the sun slide across her shoulders. On any other morning she would have welcomed it, might have hummed as she gathered the sheer embroidered curtains to each side of the east windows, would have immediately noticed her favorite peace lily drooped with thirst. But today Susan closed her eyes against the light and, determined to dissolve the disenchantment of the previous evening, began to wait. For a sign. For one good reason why her love life had taken an ironic twist. She would not move. Would not shed another tear. Would not consume as much as a crumb out of the not-quite-empty bag of Oreos left over from the night before. It was ten AM. She would give the cosmos until noon.

At ten fifteen the phone rang.

"Susan, it's me," the voice on the machine said. "Are you there? If you are, *please* pick up. Talk to me. Are you okay? I'm very worried about you."

Susan ignored the message. Again. She had nothing to say the last three times, and she had nothing to say now. The voice, whose name was Lance, had said it all. Lance. What kind of name was Lance? What mother would call her kid Lancelot Cohen? She supposed that was why he grew up thinking he had to rescue every damsel in distress. Lance, who rode in on smooth white syllables and shiny metaphors. Lance, who dazzled her with his words.

"I love you," Lance told Susan after an impassioned interlude the day before. This was not a new thing. He expressed his love often. "I love you, and I'm happier with you than I've been with anyone, but maybe this isn't working. I'm not used to so much happiness. It overwhelms me. I need some time to think. Some time apart."

*This* was new.

"Fine," Susan had said. What else could one say to an irrational person? How was she supposed to respond to being the cause of too much happiness? At forty-eight, Susan was wise to the ways of men and knew Lance's assertions were nonsense, pure and simple. Still, she wasn't going to try to cajole him into staying, or explain to him he was making a mistake. Why would she want a man who didn't want her of his own free will?

The air rippled the curtain against the slightly opened window catching Lance's lingering scent as it wafted, earthy and inviting, from Susan's pillow. She tried to ignore it, but her body had already let it in, private places warming with the memory of his touch. She searched her mind for some clue to Lance's current turn of feeling she'd missed, some prophetic hint she'd overlooked. It was true he hadn't had many long-term relationships. And the one time he'd married, seventeen years before when he was twenty-eight, it had been under questionable circumstances, and lasted less than six months.

"Her name was Jennifer," Lance had said. "I called her Jennifer Juniper like the old Donovan song."

"Did you love her?"

"Yes. But I don't think she loved me. Not the way I hoped she would." Lance's eyes had drifted in the direction of memory. "She wound up leaving me for a former lover."

"Why did you marry her?"

"She needed someone," Lance replied, as if that had explained everything.

Lancelot to the rescue.

Susan contemplated what Lance might have thought needed rescuing in her when they'd met four months before. She first noticed him in a neighborhood video store. They didn't speak, but the sensual disarray of his golden brown hair and the gray-blue of his eyes held the promise of a poetic mind. Susan didn't know exactly why a poetic mind mattered to her, but it did. She found herself drawn to a man who surprised and touched her with his words. Maybe it had to do with Beauty and

Truth, that inner resonance that made her cells sing; or how a certain turn of phrase, like the perfect ending of a poem, left something larger to enter into, something rich with possibility. Or maybe she'd simply had her fill of the trite and superficial verbal meandering that so often passed for intimate conversation. Whatever the reason, a man with a poetic mind could dissolve her defenses in a heartbeat.

Three days later, when she and Lance again ran into each other at the video store, they slipped easily into conversation and Susan had not been disappointed. She was returning a copy of *Camille Claudel* when Lance approached her.

"I think her work is far more passionate than Rodin's," he'd said.

"You know this film?" Susan was taken by the fact Lance had been familiar with the nineteenth century French sculptress.

"I've seen it twice. I think Rodin's self-centeredness played more than a delusionary part in her tragic breakdown." Lance's voice was round and melodic and filled with surprises. "Men can be very intimidated by greatness in women."

"Are you speaking from experience?"

"Always," Lance replied.

He smiled, and Susan noticed the upturned edges of his mouth, the way his eyes, catching light, became translucent. She'd let them softly enter hers; felt them slide into formless, secret spaces few had been allowed to penetrate.

"Have lunch with me," Lance said. It was a question and not a question; a seamless summoning.

"I'd like that." Susan had been beyond pretending she

64

wasn't interested, or needed to check her social calendar, or hadn't already fallen more than a little under Lance's spell. "Do you often look for dates at Blue Ridge Video?"

"I'm almost always involved with someone."

Now Susan remembered how he'd seemed embarrassed or perhaps saddened by the fact that at the time he was unattached. Maybe that was it, she thought. Maybe Lance had needed someone to rescue *him*. Or maybe not. She wasn't sure.

*This entire situation is ridiculous!* Susan aimed her silent words at any sympathetic apparition who might be listening. A gust of autumn wind replied, rustling the fiery leaves on the maple outside her window. When she'd met Lance, she hadn't even been looking. She'd grown content with the solitary life of a painter. It gave her the freedom to spend stretches of time alone, or in contemplation; to work in her studio at odd hours of the day or night.

Besides, relationships were not Susan's most accomplished arena. She'd experienced disappointment more than once in romantic liaisons and felt she'd failed twice at marriage—the first time for loving herself too little; the second for loving her husband too much, dissolving herself so into him that when he died suddenly, she felt there was nothing left of her. She'd thought it best to work out a balance before involving herself too deeply with anyone else.

Then came Lance, a man who mirrored her own heart and wit and passion. "I want you," Susan had said, making love with him one summer twilight.

"I am you," Lance whispered, melting into her so she hardly

knew where she ended and he began. Sometimes even their obscure thoughts synchronized.

"Let's plan a trip to NY," Lance said, out of the blue."

"How do you do that?" Susan replied. "I swear I was thinking that exact thing."

Twice they simultaneously jolted awake in each other's arms, startled by the same dream.

And Lance inspired Susan to push the boundaries of herself and her art. A photographer, he not only had a perceptive outer eye, but the uncanny ability to see beneath the surface of things.

"You're holding back," he'd say. "Right here, in these strokes, these colors." He'd circle his hand directly over the area she'd been struggling with. "It's too controlled. Your work is visionary, don't be afraid to break with form. Let go. Let it be what it wants to."

And Susan found when she quieted her artistic ego and got out of her own way, whole inner landscapes opened up spilling themselves sumptuously onto her canvas.

So now it comes to this, she thought, a magical affinity ending because Lancelot Cohen thinks it's too fucking good.

Susan could see the clock without moving. It was only 10:53 and her left foot was already falling asleep. *Damn!* she almost said out loud, but managed not to budge. *If Ghandi could do it, so can I.* She became arrogant in her suffering. *Breathe*, she told herself. *Just breathe*. She began to relax, but her momentary peace was interrupted by the familiar voice of guilt. *You should be working,* it said. Susan ignored it. She was busy. She was waiting, with numb feet and a battered heart, to make sense out of something senseless. Waiting. Silent as a dormouse. Still as a possum.

"What do you get when you cross a possum and a raccoon," Lance had said one evening as they held each other by firelight, sipping wine, contemplating such possibilities.

"What?" Susan replied on cue.

"A possoon."

How they had laughed at their silliness.

"What do you get when you cross an elephant and a rhinoceros?" Susan said.

"What?" Lance replied.

"An elephoceros."

"Or a rhinophant," Lance joked.

But now the joke was over and it felt as if it had been on her.

What do you get when you cross a Susan with a Lance? she thought. Pierced through the heart.

Susan continued her waiting, solid in the body she had worn well for forty-eight years. She once figured out that forty-eight years came to twenty-five million two hundred forty-six thousand and eighty minutes. That's a lot of ticks around the universal clock. Perhaps she was running out of time.

Maybe he doesn't find me attractive enough, Susan caught herself thinking, even though she knew better than to go there. Maybe he finds my nose too long or my hair and eyes too commonly brown. She contemplated her full breasts, which, though still shapely, had lost the battle against gravity, and her belly which had grown slightly rounded. She imagined that

Lance, though forty-five, preferred younger women for whom the descent of time still went unnoticed. Susan focused her mind along the six inch scar just below where a bikini would ride. It was thin, silvery and translucent, turned up on one side, down on the other like a tragi-comic metaphor for her life. And it was unevenly indented so that when she stood up, the skin above it pooched out, especially on the comic side.

"We had to widen the incision in order to remove the misshapen uterus," her seven-and-a-half-month pregnant surgeon had explained. "I wish I'd had my camera so you could see a picture of it. The fibroids formed the most unusual shape."

Susan was infinitely grateful there had been no Polaroid available in the O.R. three years before. She could not have borne to look upon the dead, barren thing which, out of a certain kind of emptiness, she had grown inside her womb.

She was once told that two things could be created out of such an emptiness—children and art—but there came a time when Susan could create neither. Paul-Henri, her second husband, the man she loved too much, was the only man with whom she had ever considered having a child. Nine years before, however, when he had been ripped from her in an arbitrary instant, his heart simply ceasing to beat, the possibility of both children and art died with him. What grew instead was a fibrous mass that fed off her emptiness, swelling into something which, although measured in terms of a life—"the fibroids are the size of a fourteen week pregnancy"—was not. Only with great determination had she learned to embrace this creative emptiness, to understand it as the space of infinite potential, and again grow her art.

In her best moments, however, Susan knew when it came to attraction, appearances could be deceiving and what drew people to each other was not always visible. Despite the fact he had had younger lovers, Lance still wanted to lie closely beside her in sunlight, still loved to caress her collarbone and place soft kisses upon her shoulders, still sweetly woke her in the night just to see her smile.

The first time they had slept together, Susan asked Lance if he was squeamish about surgical scars. In reply, he played his smooth cheek along her breasts, her belly. Gazing directly at the remnant of a wound that marked more than just her body, he gently traced his fingers over its width. Tenderly, he bent and placed his lips against it as if it were something beautiful and holy. "There's no part of you I can't love," he'd said.

No, Susan assured herself, this breakup was not about the shape of her body, but about a man who was disturbed by feeling too good.

By 11:30, Susan gave up sitting still. The breeze had turned the room chilly. Her back ached, and her bladder was full. She slowly stretched her legs and reached for the soft green blanket at the foot of the bed. She wrapped it around her and headed for the bathroom, then into the kitchen. She craved food. Rich food. Fat or sugar or chocolate food. Forbidden, exotic food. She pondered why it was women ate when they felt rejected, as if calories could fill the hollow left by a truant lover. She opened the refrigerator. Her indulgences from the night before were gone, and there wasn't much to choose from. Up until yesterday, her love life felt abundant; she'd had little need for superfluous sweets.

Susan took out a quart container of vanilla yogurt and poured a large serving into a bowl. She added granola, blueberries, almonds, and real maple syrup. For a while, the tart creamy sweet crunchiness seemed a satisfying diversion. But when Susan put the bowl in the sink, she noticed the unwashed coffee cup Lance had used the day before, and felt a hunger no amount of food could fill. She picked it up by the handle where his hand had been, pressed her lips to the place along the rim where his lips had been. *Foolish man*, she whispered.

Susan turned on the faucet and began to slowly wash the dishes. The warm sudsy water felt calming on her skin. Maybe I'm being too hard on him, she thought. She'd been ignoring Lance's phone calls since the night before. The surprise of his rejection had hit like a cyclone, turning her inside out. She felt shattered by the whirlwind of confusion and grief his words whipped up. She hadn't expected to feel that much love, that much loss, that much anger. She hadn't expected to cry that hard.

As soon as Susan walked back to the bedroom, the phone rang again.

"Please pick up. I know you're there." Pause. Susan watched Lance's words mysteriously attach themselves to a tape. "Okay," he continued, "don't pick up, but at least listen to me. I have things I need to say." Another pause. Lance seemed to be gathering his thoughts. "I'm sorry, Susan. I'm a totally insensitive and insane person. I'm miserable without you. Yet, when I'm with you, I'm so happy I become frightened by my own happiness, which also makes me miserable. Help me, Susan. I need you to help me with this."

With what? she thought. Is he asking me to help him *not* to feel happy? Susan made an impulsive motion toward the receiver, then changed her mind. She didn't know what to say. She wasn't even sure what would still be possible. If she continued with Lance, would he bolt again at the first sign of impending bliss?

"It's not you, sweetheart, it's me," the voice insisted. "It's because of me."

"And that's supposed to make me feel better?" she said to the air. It sounded to her like the typical male copout, a convenient tactic for avoiding change.

The disembodied voice continued. "I know my patterns; I know my shortcomings."

"Ha! I was right!" Susan shouted, but a second later, the shadow of Lance's words again rolled over her. No matter how cleverly he had once put them together, now they all seemed to spell disappointment. Susan reached for the bag of Oreo cookies on the night stand. There were two hiding at the bottom. She took one out and leaving it sandwiched together, defiantly consumed the wafers and cream all in one piece.

"I'm afraid you'll expect more of me than I can give," the voice went on. "I'm afraid of hurting you. I'm afraid of hurting me."

"He can't get away with this." Susan paced back and forth across the creaky bedroom floor. The room was a mess, clothing and tissues randomly tossed. The wilted lily screamed at her from its too sunny corner. She pretended not to notice. Taking the blame did *not* get him off the hook. And letting fear threaten everything wonderful they'd begun to build together was the act of a coward. Did he think she wasn't afraid? Did he think there weren't moments when she, too, felt overwhelmed?

"A rare and precious gift" Lance had called their relationship. Is that what you do with a gift? She felt he was giving her back, returning her, maybe exchanging her, acting as if he no longer wanted the jewel of her. Nothing terrible had happened. There had been no argument, no waning of passion, no lessening of love. Susan wondered if he'd ended his other relationships this way. She stopped pacing and folded herself knees to chest on the plush oriental rug. She cocooned herself in her green blanket.

"Give me a reason, Lance. Give me one true reason for this insanity."

It was as if Lance had anticipated her question. "I'm an absurdity, Susan. I'm a possoon. The raccoon part of me wants to explore everything, even though I usually make a mess, and the possum part of me wants to pull in and play dead. What can I do, Susie? Say there's hope for us." Silence. Then, "Well, I better hang up now. I *love* you. *Please* call me." He sounded pathetic.

Susan didn't know whether to laugh or cry, so she did both. Her weeping came in fits, broken apart by growing laughter which softened the edges of her anguish, rounding them into compassion. She knew it did no good to continue fighting her feelings. Maybe their relationship *would* ultimately end in disaster, but how could she live with herself if she didn't allow Lance the opportunity to make amends? Despite her saner judgment, she couldn't help but adore a man who could think up something so preposterous. Perhaps love was senseless, amorphous, unpredictable; ecstatic one minute, wretched the next, exposing the best and the worst in those who let themselves free-fall into it. And maybe she, too, was an absurdity, because suddenly Susan felt she could forgive Lancelot Cohen anything.

Of course she would call him, but not yet. There were things she wanted to think through. Although love might be senseless, it didn't have to be mindless. She walked over to the dresser, dipped a tissue in a jar of cold cream and wiped away her lipstick heart. Then slipping into jeans and a T-shirt, she anchored her hair in a ponytail. She picked up the scattered balls of tissue and the empty ice cream container from the floor by her bed, threw them in the waste basket. Digging into the bottom of the cellophane for the last Oreo, Susan carefully slid it apart this time, slowly savoring first the cream, then each chocolate wafer. A possoon, she thought, as she headed upstairs to her studio. Now *there* was an original excuse.

# RETHINKING MAX

When Lucy Minelli turned thirty-eight, her mother reminded her she was no great beauty. Judging from the absurd men who sporadically paraded through her life, Lucy thought her mother must be right. Her recent dating history read like a *Who's Who* of men on the edge. There was Bernard, who reminded her of Stewie Arugalano, a nerdy kid in her junior high school history class who could curl his ears in on themselves. The top part became wedged in the opening, the folded ear corners sticking out like perogi. Even though Bernard's ears seemed relatively well anchored, the ungraceful rest of him gave the phrase "cruel cosmic joke" new meaning. And there was Sidney who suffered from the need to apologize for everything—the over-cautious way he drove, the local weather, the starving children in Africa.

But it was after Floyd that Lucy decided men weren't worth the effort. At first, there was something about the way he'd called her "Looseee Huneee" she found downright sexy. Floyd, however, had a thang for a certain country singer, and at a precipitous moment, he whipped out three feet of Dolly Parton wig and tried to cajole her into wearing it.

"Come on, Babydoll, please put it on for me," he begged, his cheeks flushed with excitement. "I...ya know...*need* you to wear it."

Lucy'd backed away, reached for the skirt and sweater Floyd had already peeled from her body. "I suppose next you'll want me to have breast implants," she said, heading for the door.

"Only if you *want* to, Sugarpie."

It was too depressing, and Lucy soon found herself often taking refuge in fantasy. *Be careful what you wish for* some part of her cautioned. But Lucy hadn't been careful. They were *her* musings and she pushed their limits, a reasonable thing to do to escape a love life filled with disappointment. In fantasy, Lucy could avoid the pitfalls of human fallibility. Her lover could be anything she wanted him to be. The Romeo to her Juliet. The Tristan to her Isolde. The Adonis to her Aphrodite. Wait, she thought. Didn't all those affairs end in tragedy? So in her imagination, Lucy resolved to move beyond the possibility of poisons or betrayals or boar wounds. In her imagination, there would be only singular bliss.

Lucy found the notion of creating her perfect lover titillating. She contemplated identities for him. She tried

Seriozha, a name she loved the sound of. But then he would have to be Russian, and she didn't want the melodramatics of Tolstoy or Pushkin in this affair. Maybe he ought to be French, she mused. *Très romantique!* Guillaume or Jean-Pierre. No, the French could be rather insensitive. She entertained the idea of an Italian. Roberto, Marcello, Giuseppe. Too intense. Too in love with love—although she thought it very romantic to be called Lucia, like the great-grandmother for whom she was named. Lucy once came across a photograph of her in a family album. She had a slender, graceful stature with smooth hair, full breasts and a child-sized waist. Lucy, with her frizzy black curls and wide hips didn't look much like her namesake, but she had inherited her great-grandmother's blue-violet eyes. She would have preferred Lucia's skinny genes.

A Snickers bar in hand, Lucy settled into her favorite recliner. She covered herself in a soft rose-colored throw and, thought by thought, began to build her perfect lover. Foreign temperament, Lucy decided, was out, so she opted for easy American charm and a solid reliable name—Max. Mindfully, she shaped how he would speak and walk and caress her, what kind of disposition and inner qualities he would possess. She rendered him carefully, balancing the blue-green of his eyes, the gold-brown of his hair, adjusting the slant of his jaw, the curve of his shoulder, adorning him with the graceful hands of a lover until he was fully formed—her very own endearingly sensitive, unswervingly devoted, eternally adoring, fantastically sexy, but nevertheless, totally insubstantial lover.

At first, Lucy created scenarios to play out. She introduced

Max to her mother who, from the shock of his blatant affection for her daughter, was finally at a loss for hurtful words. She choreographed a romantic Valentine's dinner at La Bonne Auberge—she had the *Tournedos à la Béarnaise*, Max the *Chateaubriand*. Lucy noticed how after cutting his meat, Max did not switch the fork to his right hand, a European predilection she allowed.

Soon, all Lucy had to do was think his name and she would sense Max there, always happy to be with her. And the scenarios began to take on continuity, to build upon themselves as if they had a life of their own. Once Max showed up in a shirt Lucy had never before thought of. Another time, he spoke in a way that surprised even her imagination.

Yet he was still perfectly her Max. Lucy could tell him anything, everything, and he always understood. When she expressed her most bizarre conjectures or confessed her deepest fears and longings, Max offered only support, compassion and remedy.

"I've often thought chocolate could save the world," Lucy said to him after indulging in her favorite semi-sweet truffles for which he never criticized her.

"Sounds profoundly and entirely plausible to me," Max replied. In her creation, Lucy hadn't sacrificed intelligence for beauty.

"I'm feeling old and ugly. I wish I were twenty-one again," she sighed.

"To my eyes, you are ageless and only grow more radiant."

It was lovely.

Within weeks, Max's invisible presence had dropped into every aspect of Lucy's life. It became second nature for her not to roll over onto Max's side of the bed during the night. She invited him into her morning shower, letting his dreamy hands circle the scented lather on her back. She automatically set the table for two, and even bought a new coffee mug with a deep aqua glaze especially for Max. She gave it to him at breakfast, watched him pick it up, test it's weight in his hand.

"It's perfect," he said. "Thank you, my Lucia." (There was no reason Max couldn't call her Lucia.) Lucy filled the mug with their favorite hazelnut coffee. After a while, she hardly noticed he never drank it.

Like all women in love, Lucy's demeanor changed. Pheromones hovered in her air, and people in the real estate office where she worked couldn't help but notice. The men asked if she had done something different with her hair. The women, who recognized the signs, assumed her new glow came from an affair of the heart. In a quiet moment, Marguerite, one of her co-workers, pulled her aside.

"Whomever it is you're sleeping with, my dear, certainly must be doing something right. Do tell."

But Lucy didn't. She simply smiled and walked away leaving a trailing cloud of mystery in her wake.

A month into her affair with Max, Lucy noticed strange things happening. Like the day she turned on the TV and immediately heard "take it to the max." Or the time someone dialed Lucy's number asking for Max Minelli. She wondered if Max could be sending her messages. Fantasy had its reality, and at times Max felt more real than anyone, but messages didn't come from a figment of imagination. It's just coincidence, she told herself. She knew how to keep her inner and outer lives separate. In "reality" she went to work, cooked food, did laundry, interacted with friends. She did not, however, cast her pearls before anyone who might mistake them for something worthless.

Coincidence or not, Lucy wasn't about to give up Max, and one rainy Saturday, perfect for shopping, Lucy let him accompany her into department store dressing rooms. There, entirely unnoticed by those with little imagination, he placed soft kisses upon her shoulders, told her how absolutely breathtaking she looked in whatever she dared to try on. On the drive home they had a lively conversation about the pros and cons of psychotherapy, her favorite neo-classical painters, their choices for the Oscar.

"It's got to be either *Shakespeare In Love* or *Private Ryan*," Lucy said. "And I'm betting love will triumph over war. Don't you think so, darling?"

"Yes, I absolutely do. The writing was flawless, and Joe Fiennes was amazing. And I will tell you, my sweet, his words confessed the feelings of my own heart."

Lucy thought it considerate of Max not to speak the name of oh so perfect Gwyneth Paltrow whose charmed countenance, golden tresses and young sinewy body wreaked havoc with Lucy's self image. But she felt it appropriate to steal Gwyneth's best line just for Max.

"I love you beyond poetry," Lucy said.

Then, one evening two months into her new found ecstasy, Lucy was about to slip out of her work clothes when she sensed Max behind her. As her eyelids lowered, she imagined him unzipping his jeans, unbuttoning that copen blue shirt she loved. She felt his warm breath along her neck, the fire of him burning into her. He began to undress her, slowly, like he always did, with no concern for non-existent time. She'd spent $120 on intimate apparel just for Max—a slinky camisole trimmed with embroidered roses; a shimmering bra and matching panties in iridescent pink. Lingerie she was sure other lovers would have found unattractive on her body. Lingerie that drove Max wild. With his familiar touch, Lucy felt her bra unfasten, her underwear slide and fall leaving her in the freedom of naked skin. She heard Max whisper the things she loved to hear, clichüs she knew belonged only in the realm of fantasy—*I want you desperately; you are the center of my universe; I will worship you forever.*

Winding her way back to the reality in which her stomach growled, Lucy, trembling, pulled on her old sweats. But when she turned to head for the kitchen, her toe got caught on Max's black silk Armani briefs lying on the floor behind her feet.

Within days, *Pi*, the heavenly Givenchy scent that permeated Max's etheric air, appeared in her bathroom cabinet. Several times, Lucy felt a weighted hand against her cheek seconds before she fell into sleep. On occasion, she even found the toilet seat raised. And twice, she walked away from the breakfast table only to discover on her return, Max's previously full coffee mug empty.

It was seamless, this slipping through, until one morning, awakened by the sound of gentle snoring, Lucy found an entire body lying next to her. She curled at the corner of the bed hugging her pillow, nightgown anchored beneath her feet like a tent, and gazed at Max.

He was very beautiful. His eyelids fluttered like a real person having real dreams. His skin glowed with the color of summer, hair fanned across the pillow as if it had been visited by a sudden wind. Folded on his side, the moon of Max's shoulder seemed to be waiting for Lucy's familiar kiss. She bent to brush her lips against it, swept a lock of hair from his smooth face.

New breath rose and fell in Max's perfect torso. He looked like "David" come to life in Lucy's bed. A wave of earthly insecurity washed over her. Suddenly her Rubenesque disproportion seemed hardly a match for a Michaelangelo. What had she done? What she'd allowed in fantasy felt foolish and uncomfortable in practicality. She was not the Lucy she'd secretly invented herself to be.

Lucy whimpered and Max stretched. He rolled on to his back. Slowly, he opened the blue-green eyes Lucy had conceived for him. He smiled and spoke. "I want you desperately; you are the center of my universe; I will worship you forever," he said, and in the real world, Lucy knew she had a problem.

# THE VIOLET MISUNDERSTANDING

*Ce soir. À huit heures,* the man whispered into my ear, then quickly placed a small, white envelope on the table and scurried into the drizzle that had been falling steadily for an hour. I opened the unsealed note and read it. *Ma chérie,* it began. *Je compte les minutes jusqu'au moment de notre rencontre.* It was signed, *JMD*. Obviously, this stout, gray-haired messenger made a mistake. Or had he? Maybe this was the way destiny worked. You think you're marking a clever path inside your own thin skin, only to discover you really don't have a clue as to where you're going, or even who you are. One layer gets peeled away *et voila!*—you're gone.

Even though I knew the man must have been at least two blocks away, I still found myself perusing the busy café. To my left, an old woman with a bright green shawl and a yelping Lhasa apso anchored at her heels, mumbled into her coffee and croissant. In a far corner, a young couple in the throes of infatuation smiled dreamily into each other's eyes. Three tables over, two men with spiked, yellow hair were engaged in an animated conversation that rippled the surface of the damp, spring afternoon.

I'd gone to Paris to escape Daddy's hovering. After mother died eight years ago, when I was sixteen, he said I had become "out of control." Since then, he's tried to manipulate my comings and goings according to his idea of what *in* control ought to be—the "proper" schools (I've dropped out of the best—Radcliff, Vassar, Smith), the "proper" social circles (totally dull and superficial), the twice weekly visits to the "proper" Fifth Avenue shrink.

Several times he'd even attempted to convince me it might be good if I went someplace where I would be "properly" cared for while I contemplated the error of my ways. Just because *he* was able to go about his life as if the loss of the woman he once worshipped like a goddess was nothing more than a socially messy incident didn't mean I could. "An accident," he'd called it, best forgotten as soon as possible. *I* was the one who found her lying there in her favorite green silk nightgown, her bronze hair fanned across the pillow like a Pantene commercial. She was so beautiful. Despite the empty vial of Valium on the floor, it was hard to believe she was dead. For a long time, I couldn't forgive her. But Daddy simply went about his ordered routine almost as if nothing had happened. He stuffed his grief and fear and anger so far down in the family plumbing it backed up inside of me. I felt everything for both of us.

For four months I had somehow managed to be on my best behavior. No skinny-dipping in the fountain in front of The Met; no late night cavorting with aspiring Broadway gypsies, gay or otherwise; not even any unpaid parking tickets. I had also been making a diligent effort not to purposefully push anyone's buttons at my friend's Soho boutique where I helped out part-time. So I decided to reward myself, to get away from New York and go someplace *I* wanted to go. Perhaps have a little adventure. But even I couldn't have choreographed the seduction which seemed to be developing around me. It was too delicious—a strange little man seamlessly sliding a mysteriously romantic message into my dreary day. *Tonight. Eight o'clock,* he had said. And the note—*My dearest, I count the minutes until our meeting,* with an address in St. Germain, the 6th arrondissement, near the Luxembourg Gardens.

The question was, should I take JMD up on his intriguing invitation? My Paris plan went like this: If it flies in the face of logic, go for it! A risky strategy, I admit, but a hell of a lot more interesting than numbing on Prozac and trying to wedge myself into somebody else's constricted idea of what a life should be.

By seven that evening, back in my room at this quaint, boutique hotel where I was staying, my mind was made up. Of course I would go. It had been too long since I'd ventured into anything unorthodox. I opened the closet and scanned its contents. It didn't take me long to decide on a short black skirt, wide-necked pale peach sweater and low black heels. I dressed and looked in the mirror. I liked what looked back—green eyes, auburn hair, long legs, perky breasts. Not bad for a mad woman, I thought. But I wasn't stupid. I knew I could be making an appointment with real danger. What if I were being led to the lair of a rapist? Or a psychopathic killer? Or worse, someone just like my father who would lecture me to death?

If Daddy had known what I was contemplating, he really would have had me committed. But he only knew I had gone to Paris to visit Celeste, a "respectable" graphic designer who, in truth, I cared about more as an excuse than a friend. I couldn't exactly tell him I wouldn't be staying with her; and he wouldn't exactly have understood that I needed a little space of my own. So I figured, I'm almost twenty-five years old, I don't have to report to my father anymore.

A shiver washed over me as the taxi pulled up in front of a beautiful old building with wrought iron balconies in front of high, arched windows. If this person was a psychopath, I thought, at least he was a stylish one. Not that I was a stranger to affluence. Money was the one thing there was always enough of in my family. And it never bought me anything I really needed. It couldn't buy me back my mother.

After figuring out the tip, I paid the driver and walked to the tall front door. I rang the bell. The man who answered was none other than the mystery messenger, himself.

"Good evening," he said stiffly.

"It's exactly eight o'clock and I'm here." I tried to be casual about not knowing who exactly it was that had invited me.

"Very American," he said, heavily rolling his eyes along with his r's.

I was beginning to feel a little intimidated.

"*Entrez, s'il vous plait.*"

"*Merci,*" I said.

He cleared his throat.

"This way," he continued, as he led me into an elegant, but comfortable, living room with a nine foot Steinway grand occupying a good portion of it. "Monsieur Duval will be with you in a moment."

Grateful this somber little man was not my host, I tried to relax. I looked around. I noticed an unusual, hand-blown glass sculpture on a pedestal, and a Rauschenberg reaching high over the wide mantel. Having been schooled in ostentation, pricey art was one thing I knew something about. Too nervous to settle back, I sat propped at the edge of one of the two cream-colored, textured silk sofas that faced each other across a low marble table in front of the fireplace. I surmised Monsieur Duval must know whomever he had sent the invitation to and shuddered at the prospect of how he might react when he found me in her place.

I had barely begun to contemplate how I would explain myself, when I heard hesitant footsteps vibrating the surface of the polished oak floor in the hallway. Five seconds later, "he" entered the room.

"*Bonsoir.* Good evening."

"Good evening," I echoed.

M. Duval appeared to be maybe thirty-four or five, tallish, with a slender, well-proportioned physique. He was dressed in linen slacks and a softly draped silk shirt. His eyes were dark, his sleek, deep brown hair pulled back into a tail. And he moved with a sensuality that kept me glued to his every gesture.

"You are much younger than I thought you would be for one who writes to me with such passion," he said, with a French accent to die for.

"I'm an old soul," I said. I managed a smile, but I was becoming more confused by the second. How was it that M. Duval believed he knew me, thought I had actually written things to him, and yet did not recognize me as an impostor? I was beginning to suspect that either Prozac withdrawal was causing hallucinations, or I had somehow taken a turn into *Le Twilight Zone Français*.

"Monsieur Duval..." I began, thinking perhaps it was best to confess everything.

"Please," he interrupted, "call me *Jean-Michel*."

Jean-Michel was one of those names that sounded better in French than it did in English. I would not particularly have liked calling him John-Michael, but I thought *Jean-Michel* suited him perfectly.

"Jean-Michel," I began again, impulsively changing my strategy, carefully weighing my words so as not to give away what I should, but did not, know. "You have a lovely home." God, I sounded like those pompous social snobs I knew who, while giving a compliment, were simultaneously taking inventory to see how they measured up.

"*Merci*," he replied. "I am touring so much these days, I am not able to enjoy it very often. These last weeks in Paris have been a much needed rest for me."

*Touring.* My eyes shifted to the grand piano. He must be a concert pianist. Then it hit me. *Jean-Michel Duval!* He was to classical piano what Baryshnikov was to the ballet, and *I* had landed myself smack in the middle of his living room. It was priceless. Wait until my friends back home hear about this one, I thought.

Following my gaze, Jean-Michel glided over to the ebony bench and sat. Before I knew it, the haunting sounds of Chopin exhaled through his fingers. It was exquisite, and I thought it had to have been his playing that inspired the mystery woman to write to him.

"I remember what it means to you," he said sweetly, as he walked back toward me, "*ze* Nocturne in D-Flat."

"Yes," I replied, sticking to one syllable words whenever possible. Besides not wanting to commit a *faux pas,* I had learned how much a man will reveal if a woman keeps her conversation to a minimum.

"I remember that it was the first thing you had heard me play." Jean-Michel paused. "Now I will tell you that the poetry which described your feelings changed forever the way I have played it since. You have become my secret Muse," he said, caressing my face with his eyes as he eased himself onto the sofa opposite mine. "But forgive me. I have prepared some champagne."

"No. Thank you," I said.

He looked a little surprised. I needed all my wits about me. I was beginning to feel I might be heading for disaster and wondered where in the world I could go from there. I opted for a change of direction.

"What made you invite me here tonight?" I said.

He seemed confused. "But it was *you* who finally agreed to see me, *n'est-ce pas*? *Mercredi*, you wrote. *Le vingt-trois Avril. Quatre heure et demie de l'après midi au Café du Cygne. Avec des violettes dans mes cheveux,*. Although the mistake in the date concerned me. Today is Wednesday, but it is the *22nd*, not the 23rd. I wasn't sure which you meant, the day or the date."

I had to think fast. "Oh," I said, hoping I was not about to sink deeper. "Yes, I'm sorry. I'm not used to writing in French, and I realized my error too late."

"Not too late," Jean-Michel replied. "You are here. And if you had not come, I would have tried, myself, to find you tomorrow." He looked hard into my eyes. "Nothing could have kept me from this *rendez-vous*."

I finally understood why I'd been approached in the first place. *With violets in my hair*, her note had said. The violets I had impulsively bought and tucked behind my ear instigated this entire misunderstanding. And I surmised by now that our mystery woman had written more than just fan letters.

"Amelia," Jean-Michel began, using "her" name for the first time. "I think I am in love with you."

When will you know for sure? I thought. Sarcasm was a convenient tactic for avoiding the more painful question I couldn't help asking myself—When was the last time someone told *you* he loved you, Alex? Someone with his clothes on? But well-trained in camouflaging my emotions, I quickly pulled back to the situation at hand. This had become serious. "Amelia" may have been waiting her entire life to hear those words.

To buy time, I got up and strolled across the room with no particular destination. Jean-Michel followed, moving gracefully toward me. He faced me and locked onto my uneasy gaze coming closer and closer until there was barely space between us for breath. Despite the fact he was a total stranger to me, my knees felt weak and those familiar butterflies fluttered themselves into a frenzy in my stomach. He took me gently by the shoulders and kissed me. Extravagantly. It was sensational, I admit, yet I knew I did not feel what Amelia would have.

Seeing where this might lead, I got my hormones under control and decided I had better make an exit. Under the circumstances, my Paris plan needed some modification. It also seemed I was beginning to grow a conscience, and a tug-of-war was tearing away inside me. My old self wanted to hang out a little longer, steal another kiss, pretend for just a few more minutes it was really *me* Jean-Michel loved. But my new self was beginning to feel remorse for her folly and feared the embarrassment of being exposed. She wanted out.

"Jean-Michel, please, not so quickly," I said gently. It seemed reasonable that Amelia might have expressed the same sentiment. "I really must go."

"Amelia, I am sorry if I displeased you," he said.

"No, no. You pleased me very much," I replied. At least that was not a lie. "I just prefer not to move so fast."

"Of course. I should have realized." He looked as if he might cry. "I'll see you out." Jean-Michel walked me to door and softly pressed his lips to each of my cheeks. "Shall I call you a taxi?"

"No, thank you. I'd like to walk a little. I'll be fine."

"I must see you again," he said. "Where are you staying?"

"I'll contact you," I replied. He stared at me as if he needed more reassurance. "I promise."

All that night I lay awake feeling wretched about what I had done. I couldn't get the pathetic look of disappointment on Jean-Michel's face out of my mind. You really screwed up this time, Alex, I told myself. I may act a little bizarre now and then, but, contrary to what my father might believe, I am not hard-hearted. I just keep the soft parts well protected against bruising. Jean-Michel and Amelia were obviously important to each other, cared very much for each other, and I felt as if I had— even if unintentionally—used their history for my own demented entertainment. It was the first time in a very long while I was obsessively concerned about somebody else. It wasn't altogether a bad feeling.

I became set on finding Amelia and hopefully absolving myself in the process. She had made a mistake in the date, I reasoned. Perhaps she still thought she had written "Thursday," and would be waiting that afternoon. I would look for her and explain everything.

By the time I got to The Swan Cafй it was four-fifteen. I

found a table, ordered a *café au lait,* and began to  look around. Almost immediately, a woman who appeared to be in her early thirties, dressed in a soft, flowy skirt and lavender sweater walked up and took a table close by. Anchored to one side of her dark, stylish hair was a small cluster of violets. I approached her.

"Amelia?" I said.

She looked at me as if searching her mind for how we might know each other. "Yes? *Oui?*" she replied, cautiously.

I continued in English. "We haven't exactly met," I explained. "May I sit down for a minute?"

"Well, I'm expecting someone shortly."

"That's sort of what I'm here to talk to you about."

"Did Jean-Michel send you?"

"No. Not exactly." She invited me to sit, and I then began to explain, as best I could, what had happened the day before. I hadn't quite finished when Amelia lashed out.

"So, let me get this straight! You're saying you let Jean-Michel believe that *you* were *me*! How could you?" she said, rather loudly, drawing the attention of the people around us, her body tensing, perhaps suppressing an urge to scratch my eyes out.

"I don't know," I said, with a surprising calmness born, I guess, of owning that *I* was the one who had started this whole thing. I was used to being blamed, but in this case, I really had earned the consequences. "He didn't seem to know many particulars about you other than that you were American, and, at first, things seemed to go smoothly."

Amelia interrupted, again. "He knows everything about me that matters! I don't even know why I'm sitting here listening to any of this," she said sharply, sliding her chair back from the table, preparing to leave.

But I knew she wouldn't.

"If you go now, you'll never know what happened," I said. "And you won't know how to find him." She hesitated, then eased back into her seat. Careful not to make anymore preconceived judgments, I continued. "After a while, when it became complicated with Jean-Michel, I just didn't know how to tell him. Without breaking his heart. I felt awful."

"What in the world possessed you to attempt this charade in the first place?" Amelia was still incensed.

Her words hit too close to home. My father could have said the same thing. I felt a surge of defensiveness begin to rumble in my solar plexus, but I was determined to maintain *sang-froid*. My new conscience felt it owed Amelia the truth. "Sometimes, I just do things like that. Insanity runs in my family," I added with, I admit, more than a hint of sarcasm. "I'm here now. I showed up to find you, didn't I?"

She took a deep breath, apparently trying to thin out some of her own anger. "I suppose that's true."

"Look, if you want to leave, fine. But if you want me to tell you the rest of the story, you're going to have to listen without attacking me after every three sentences."

She looked hard into my eyes as if she was searching for a spark of trust. "All right," she replied with an edge that sounded as if she had not totally convinced herself.

"He's really in love with you, Amelia." I was proud of myself for resisting the urge to resort to obnoxiousness.

"Whatever you've been writing to him has touched him deeply. He even played Chopin's Nocturne in D-Flat and said he remembered what it meant to you."

Amelia's icy stance suddenly melted into tears. I grabbed a few tissues from my bag and handed them to her.

"It'll never be the same, now that you've stolen our first meeting," she mumbled, mostly to herself.

She was right. It never would. "I know, Amelia. I'm sorry. I had no idea how things would develop."

We each let some silence slip between us.

"Did he...kiss you?" Amelia seemed uncertain about wanting to hear my answer.

"Yes. But I think he was disappointed. I think he could sense I did not respond in the way he had hoped. That was my cue to contrive an exit. I would never have let it go any further. Please believe me."

"I'm trying to understand what would possess a person to do what you've done," Amelia sighed, still weeping. "You've ruined everything."

"It's hard to explain, but every once in a while, I need to do something totally unreasonable."

Amelia looked at me as if she was stretching to see if there was any part of her that could identify with what I had confessed.

"I know you don't owe me any explanations, but would you mind if I asked you some things?

"You're right. I *don't* owe you any explanations."

"Please, Amelia. So much was left unexplained."

She seemed to weigh her thoughts before responding.

"What do you want to know?"

"How is it that you and Jean-Michel have never met, yet are in love?"

Amelia took time before answering. "All I've ever known was that *I* loved Jean-Michel. I hardly dared to imagine he could love me back. Yet now, you're telling me he does."

"I'm certain of it."

Amelia's expression turned wistful. "I grew up surrounded by great music. My grandfather was first violin with the New York Philharmonic, but after he died, little by little more mundane things claimed my attention—my personal dramas, my work."

"What kind of work?" I was surprised to find I was interested, that I actually liked Amelia.

"I'm an editor for a small publishing house."

Something between us seemed to have shifted and Amelia now spoke in a normal tone of voice. I surmised she probably needed *someone* to talk to and I had been elected.

"I used to write stories and poetry of my own," she continued, "but I let my writing, like my love of music, fall by the wayside. Until a year ago."

"Jean-Michel?"

"Yes. Jean-Michel. It was quite by accident. One day, I flipped on the radio and heard someone playing the Chopin Opus 27 No. 2 Nocturne in D-Flat like I'd never heard it played

95

before. I thought it the most compelling sound. Each note rang true and touched something deep within me, something I'm still not sure I completely understand."

These two belong together, I thought.

Amelia's eyes drifted off in the direction of memory. "Afterwards, I felt a compulsion to find this man with the angelic hands, almost as if some palpable significance pulled me toward him. I don't think we always have conscious choice when it comes to love. I think some people are just our destiny."

"I've never been in love," I said. If I never admitted to loving anyone, then no one could ever *not* love me back. At least, that was my reasoning.

"It's not an easy thing to love under circumstances few can understand," Amelia continued.

"You mean people thinking you're just another woman with the hots for a famous pair of hands?"

"Exactly."

I had a shining moment.

"So what happened?" I said.

"I had to wait three months until Jean-Michel was scheduled to play again in New York. Meanwhile, I read all I could find about him—articles, interviews, reviews. And I listened to all of his tapes and CD's."

Amelia was still in a sort of reverie, and I wasn't sure I was entirely comfortable with listening to her profoundly serious confessions. No one had ever confided in me as an adult before. "I still don't understand," I said. "How did you two get to where you are now?"

"I only meant to leave one letter backstage after that first performance, but I found myself attending concert after concert whenever and wherever I could, and each time, my feelings for Jean-Michel and his music grew into grander and grander expression. It was as if we nourished each other through our art. I gave the largest of myself to him through my letters. I knew he understood every word and all that was between and beneath them. I felt it reflected back to me in his playing."

"So, why did you wait so long to reveal yourself to him in person?"

"It's strange, but in a way I was afraid it would spoil everything, that if we faced each other as just Amelia and Jean-Michel, somehow the magic we had built between us would shatter into unrecognizable fragments. I still had connections in the music world. I could easily have gotten an invitation to meet him, but I was afraid of being disappointed. A great artistic gift alone does not make someone inherently more worth loving. There are too many inspired artists who are less than inspiring human beings."

"I don't think you'll be disappointed."

She didn't reply.

"So why now, Amelia?"

"I guess I knew I had to face the music." Amelia smiled for the first time, her serious demeanor totally transformed. I couldn't help but feel a twinge of jealousy in the presence of such metamorphosis. With her fine bones and engaging blue eyes, I was sure Jean-Michel would find her irresistible. "You know, I didn't even ask you your name," she said.

"It's Alex."

"So, Alex, how did you leave off with Jean-Michel?"

"I told him I would contact him. If you want me to, I'll confess everything, apologize and suffer the consequences."

"No. I think you've done enough," she said, gently this time. "I'll handle it from here. In my own way. If you'll please give me his address."

"Will you let me know what happens?"

"I don't know."

"I don't think I could bear believing I've caused irreparable damage," I said.

She hesitated. "All right. I'll let you know."

"No matter what?"

"I suppose so."

I wrote Jean-Michel's address along with mine on a napkin and gave it to Amelia. "

Again, I'm so sorry," I said. "*Bonne chance!*" I added, anxious to take my tired self back to my room and sort through the remnants of this mad adventure.


That evening, I decided not to go out with Celeste as I had planned. I called her and told her I'd see her the following afternoon. I needed to contemplate what had happened. I knew I'd done the honorable thing, but I still wondered if Jean-Michel ever could have loved *me*, Alexandra Strasser. I wondered if any man could, especially without my usual twenty-seven layers of emotional armor. I thought how uncanny it was that all the pieces, like seemingly isolated melodies, blended harmoniously together—both Amelia and I being American, the violets, the wrong date, which made it possible to set the whole thing right. It felt hopeful.

Two days later, I received a note from Amelia. It said—*I have faced the music and it has embraced me!*

*Moi aussi*, I thought. Me, too.

# THE EX-LOVER, THE NURSE, AND THE DATE

Kira arrives at the restaurant early. She gives The Date's description to the hostess, asks that he please be directed to her table. It is not her idea to be there, but The Friend's insistence that, after the recent turn of events, Kira needed to "get her emotional butt back in the saddle."

For weeks now, Kira's had plans to fly from North Carolina to Colorado to visit her Ex-Lover with whom she is still close, but a few days ago he called to tell her he knows the timing sucks, it really sucks, but he's became totally smitten with a proctology nurse and things are moving fast.

Kira now sees The Date coming toward her. He's about 5' 9" wearing a blue nylon jogging jacket, a grey crinkled button down shirt, saggy low-riding jeans and white *Nikes*. In person, his hair is thinner than it appears in his photo. And wilder. Tufts swirl defiantly, puff out perpendicular to his pink scalp.

Kira wonders why she listened to The Friend and jumped back into online dating. Memories of her initial venture in that arena, before she'd finally found The Ex-Lover, were the stuff of nightmares. Grown men called themselves *Pooterface, Lover4U, Cuddlebuns.* Many displayed photos posed against their motorcycles or Jaguars. One posted a picture taken in drag. A fifty-nine-year-old heterosexual in a teased blond wig wearing a flowered housedress with dark chest hair frothing at the neckline is not a pretty sight. Another put the face of his slobbering bulldog in place of his own.

Kira had written to a few men in whom she thought she might be interested, but wound up meeting with only one who lived close by. His name was Sven. He played the mandolin. Two years younger than she, he was tall, with a straggly gray ponytail. He dressed in a T-shirt and jeans. As soon as he saw her, she could read the disappointment in his eyes. She was sure he was hoping for someone with more youth and curve. By the end of their half-hour meeting, they'd agreed it wasn't working. The next time Kira went online, she noticed Sven had changed his profile, lowered the age of his ideal date to read: *from 25 to 39.*

Emails had rolled in regularly. Some were over the top. *NeoPsych* wrote: *Just can't help it. I see your smile and break out in an uncontrollable paroxysmal and parhelic smile, thinking of sprites, spirits, and sylphs. Thank you.*

Other messages were downright obnoxious. *You've been*

*online almost a month now. PLENTY of time to find the love of your life amidst all those HUNDREDS of profiles, right? I bookmarked your profile because it was farily clear to me that online dating would most likely be a disappointing experience for you. If I'm wrong and you are just having the best time of your entire life—well, I guess you can stop reading now...*

A twenty-nine year old man in Ohio who, seeming to ignore the fact that Kira was not likely to be interested in someone young enough to be her son, asked: *Is the distance a deal breaker?*

But by far the most brazen response had been from a farmer and self-professed poet who began: *As far as poetry goes...I'll show ya mine, if, you show me yours* — then went on to unwind a twenty-four line ode of sorts, containing sentiments such as *For love is not like a pickle, that will make you tickle, while thou art all alone...*followed by the directive: *Ok, strip...your turn!*

To get The Friend off her case, Kira had reactivated her old profile and signed up for a free trial period. She did a fifty mile search, checked out the lineup. It had been almost two years since she'd first explored online dating, yet she found mostly the usual suspects. There was one face, however, she hadn't seen before, someone new in town. His profile said he was fifty-five, average build. He'd checked post-graduate education. He had silver hair, fair skin, blue eyes. His only photo was a close-up taken at an angle. His smile was close-mouthed. He had a pleasant face.

Needing to do something with her mind other than

fantasize about how The Ex was fawning over The Nurse, turning on his considerable charm, seducing her with honesty, she'd written to Laithor54321, asked him the two all-important questions: Is he witty? Does he read? He wrote back. No, he doesn't read much. Despite this, they emailed for a while and Kira agreed to meet him for dinner. It's just a meal, she'd rationalized. Something to do on a Saturday night. How bad could it be?

The Date seems a lot happier to see Kira than she is to see him. He smiles. He has too many teeth for his mouth. He sits down. They look over the menu. They order and The Date launches into a monologue on what appears to be his favorite subject: himself. He's divorced, has two grown sons, is retired from twenty unhappy years with Microsoft, is needing to pay attention to his own life for a change. He came to Asheville because it was time to do some deep inner work. And to meet people he can relate to, people who can relate to him. He's never felt "ordinary."

The server finally brings the food and The Date takes an intermission in order to sample what's on his plate. Kira can't tell whether or not he likes it. For a while they eat in silence and Kira's mind is sucked back to the events of the last week.

"Do you still want me to come out," she had asked The Ex-Lover when he'd called with news of The Nurse. Her solar plexus felt like a bowling ball had been hurled through it.

"It's fine," he said.

"*FINE?*" she replied.

"Fine" was how the Ex described the Dutch Reformed

world of denial in which he'd grown up. The Land of Fine, he called it, where "fine" floated on the emotional surface of things like water lilies on a pond full of scum.

"No!" he said. "I mean yes, I want to see you. I told her all about you, about us, that we were still friends and that you were coming for a week."

"What did you tell her about *us*?"

"Everything." He paused.

Kira wondered what, exactly, "everything" included. Did he tell The Nurse how, after eight months of saying he was "so happy so happy," he suddenly decided he no longer wanted the relationship, canceled his scheduled move from Virginia to North Carolina, said they should take space in order to sort things out? And for no reason he could give other than some nebulous but all consuming fear? In a way, she hoped he hadn't been that truthful. That level of honesty would have meant The Ex-Lover already cared for The Nurse in a way which, despite Kira's efforts to move beyond it, made her jealous.

Kira had been apprehensive about what he was not saying.

"Is she young?" she asked.

"She's our age, fifty-eight."

"Is she beautiful?"

"More like...attractive."

The Ex had once thought Kira beautiful. In the largest sense it meant little, yet she couldn't help feeling a twinge of satisfaction.

The Ex-Lover met The Nurse through the same dating site on which he and Kira had met. She wished she hadn't, but after he'd moved to Colorado, Kira had looked up his revised profile. His profile name was the same—*iamrickblaine*, but other parts had changed. Describing his potential match, he'd added—*At some point she will have to be a good kisser.* Kira had spoiled him. For months The Ex told her he hadn't found anyone with whom to test that requirement. But now he had, and Kira hoped The Nurse had lips like prunes, the cleverness of stone. She hoped The Nurse loathed *Gatsby*, Gershwin, peanut butter, the *Tour de France.* She was not proud of what she felt.

"You're very quiet."

The Date's voice pulls Kira back to her present situation. She starts a new conversational thread.

"So, where did you go to school?" she asks.

"Actually, I didn't. I finished high school in the Navy. I'm self-taught. I can do practically anything."

Kira doesn't bring up the fact that he'd checked post-graduate degree on his profile. "Anything?" she says.

"Practically."

"Like what?" She tries to sound polite, interested.

"Before I moved here, I finished building stables for my sister's eleven horses. Did every single bit myself." He looks into Kira's eyes. "Carpentry, plumbing, electricity. I've built houses, a windmill, put together an entire automobile. I've grown everything from broccoli to rutabagas. I paint. I play piano, guitar, flute..."

"Did you ever write a poem?" she asks.

"Once." He smiles.

Kira tries not to stare, but she's fascinated by the forest of incisors, bicuspids, laterals, molars that sprout from between his lips.

"Once?" she says.

"When I was in high school, before I dropped out, I wrote a poem and the teacher said it was too good. She failed me, told me I must have plagiarized it. She said no one my age could write like that."

Either this guy is a genius, Kira thinks, or an arrogant fool. She watches him eat. One can learn a lot about a man by the way he eats. The Date is tentative, pushes his rice around the plate. She can't help remembering how the Ex savored a good meal, yumm'd over it, exclaimed, "This is soooo wonderful."

Kira has been trying to kick the Ex-Lover completely off the shaky pedestal on which she's kept him. Remembering things she didn't like about him helped. How he looked at her sideways through bulgy Marty Feldman eyes. How he slumped low in a chair as if trying to make himself invisible. How he stubbornly wore those old black Reeboks with worn Velcro closings that kept popping open. And there was the infamous couch.

It was not so much the thing itself...well maybe it was, but also the couch as metaphor that had disturbed her. Kira hadn't come face to face with it until Christmas vacation, three months into their relationship. After a five hour drive, she'd arrived at The Ex-Lover's apartment. He showed her around, apologized a lot.

Then she saw it, the odious couch he'd so often joked about, the one which, six years before, his ex-wife had thrown out with him. She knew his jokes had been seamed with embarrassment, loss, regret. He wore the past like a shroud around his heart.

The couch was everything The Ex-Lover had said, maybe worse. The once stylish L-shaped sectional was torn and frayed, the soft pastel colors of its fabric faded to muddy beige. There was hardly any cushioning left so that the wood frame poked through in areas and made it impossibly uncomfortable to sit on. But the most offensive part was the remnants of his three sons — food stains, trails of permanent markers that had strayed off the page, the grime of decades. Despite already knowing its history, it had been a jolt for Kira to actually encounter the nefarious piece of furniture.

But now, as Kira sits opposite The Date, listening to his inane egotistical rambling, reasons she'd been drawn to The Ex-Lover begin to surface—the way he'd slow danced with her in the middle of the dining room; Sunday afternoons at their favorite cafù, sipping coffee, discussing short stories he was teaching, movies they loved; how he peppered his conversation with little French endearments he'd learned when he taught for a year *en Provence*.

In early emails, when they were testing each other's atmosphere, The Ex-Lover had written: "Today, preparing for class, I was moved to tears by Flannery O'Connor's essays on her own work, because they were so absolutely devoid of nonsense, so full of irreducible truth."

Kira'd responded by asking for an irreducible truth about him.

His reply: "I am the best listener you will ever find."

For the three months after their relationship ended, Kira and The Ex had had no communication. But, later, when she'd felt compelled to write to him, to see how he was doing, he'd responded warmly. Soon they began exchanging emails regularly, visited a couple of times.

And when The Ex-Lover told her he was moving to Colorado, they'd agreed to stay in touch. Up until the appearance of The Nurse, they'd written often, talked once or twice a week.

Since The Ex had called with the news that his love life was whizzing right along, Kira has felt him pulling away. She knows he needs to do this. She realizes she's looked to him too much to fill an emptiness. And lately it has occurred to her that even early on, there were signs of their imminent end. Besides their only Valentine's Day having been marred by separation and disaster—The Ex-Lover calling to say he wouldn't be coming, he'd had a biking accident, had rammed his head into a parked truck—Kira had discovered that no photographs had ever been taken of the two of them together. And when The Ex had inscribed a copy of Italo Calvino's *If On A Winter's Night A Traveler* for her birthday, he'd mistakenly used a lead pencil instead of a pen, so that the *great love* and *plenty of affection* he'd addressed to her *amazing* self, was as impermanent as he proved to be.

The Date now leans a little closer. "I already feel like you understand things most people don't," he says.

Kira's not sure this is a good thing.

He looks around the room as if to see if people are watching. "I don't tell this to everyone," he begins, then stops abruptly as the server approaches and removes their plates. They order tea and coffee, no dessert.

The Date continues. "I'm not from here."

"You're from Raleigh, I know," Kira says, but already she suspects he's not talking about terrestrial geography.

"I mean I'm not from…Earth."

"Oh," she says. "From where, then?"

"From…off planet."

"Like Mars?"

"Venus actually."

The Date seems to be waiting to see Kira's reaction. She offers none.

He goes on. "At least that's where my soul replacement is from."

The theme from *The Twilight Zone* runs through Kira's mind.

"There's more," The Date says.

"What's that?"

He takes off his glasses, wipes new sweat from his brow. "I haven't told anyone this yet," he says.

Lucky me, she thinks.

The Date continues. "Laithor, my interplanetary liaison came to me and explained my real mission here on earth."

Water now seems to be pouring off The Date's forehead, down the sides of his flushed cheeks, his neck. His skin looks clammy and red. Kira fears he is about to have some kind of seizure.

"Are you all right?" she asks. She wonders if anyone else has noticed his condition.

"Yes. The hot flashes will be over soon." He takes a long pause. "Right after I birth the Tri-Lobals."

"The what?"

"Shhhh," he says. Again, he cautiously looks around. "The Tri-Lobal Venusian Interlings," whispers The Date. "You know," he says, "to save planet earth."


It's almost ten when Kira gets home. She immediately turns on the computer and removes all cyber traces of herself from the online dating site. Nothing like dinner with a Venusian to put things into perspective. Her suitcase is still lying open on the bedroom chair, clothing for Colorado layered inside—sweaters, her favorite black skirt, a long red scarf. Kira is scheduled to leave in a week, and even though she emailed The Ex-Lover three days ago asking if he really still wants her to come, there's been no reply.

She's sure The Ex is procrastinating, afraid her visit will ruin things between him and The Nurse, but doesn't know how to tell her. Most men have the emotional courage of a parsnip.

Kira changes into sweats, begins an email to him saying she's decided not to come. As usual, she rescues him. *You can relax now*, she adds at the end, *I've taken you off the hook*. She's about to click send when the phone rings.

"Hi," he says, "it's me."

At the sound of The Ex's voice, Kira's throat tightens, pushes almost into tears.

"I was just writing to you," she says.

"What were you writing?"

"That I'm not coming out."

"I think it's best," he says. "That's why I called." There is sadness in his voice. "I'm sorry it's taken me so long to respond. I didn't know how to tell you."

Reaching for a tissue, Kira blots the tears now trickling down her cheek. "It's Valentine's Day," she says.

"I know." He hesitates. "Well...I just wanted to tell you over the phone, rather than write."

Kira lets a long silence stretch between them.

"I love you," he says.

"Yes," she replies.

Kira gets up and slowly paces the room. She wants The Ex-Lover out of her thoughts, out of her heart, yet the larger part of her knows the pain is not about him, but about her own fears — the fear he was her last chance, that at her age there may be no one else, the fear of her own loneliness. And she's jealous, not of The Nurse, but of the passion The Ex-Lover must be feeling, the connection and exhilaration of romance, new love, infinite promise.

Securing her frizzy auburn hair in a scrunchie, Kira gets on the treadmill housed in the far corner of the room. Starting slowly, she builds speed attempting to out-run the doubts and questions that circle her mind. She knows it's time to let go of what was, to move forward with her life. She knows what she must do.

When sufficiently exhausted, Kira lights a black candle, turns The Ex-Lover's photo face down, goes to the computer, and with one great ceremonious sweep of the mouse, deletes the folder containing their 1,537 emails.

# The Impermanence of Eagles

He rode in with the seasons, dropped his smile, his words, his blues into her life, casually, as if small pieces were enough, as if a verse, a touch, a word could fill the lonely hollow of a heart.

She'd known him first in summer, curls cropped short, his cheeks flushed by mountain air and sun. He sat alone beneath a sycamore, making music, a slant of light around him like a halo, like a ghost.

In autumn, his skin turned fair, those summer linen shirts he'd worn—sleeves rolled up, buttons opened to reveal that place between his collarbones—now topped by leather, black and butter soft. She measured distance by his songs, waited seasons just to hear him laugh.

She saw him last in winter warmed by firelight and longing.

He'd stopped en route to see some friends. To come so far he needed reasons other than his heart. Still in stocking feet, no lipstick on, she heard the doorbell ring. Weekend bag over one shoulder, guitar across the other, his smile reached back to autumn.

"How could I have gone so long without seeing you," he'd said, embracing her, whispering how much he missed her. He kissed her deeply, held her with the weight of truth, told her she was lovelier than paradise.

They went to eat, richly, as always. That time French, with deep red wine and candlelight. Only for an instant would he let her touch his hand, out, where anyone might see. Yet riding home, seamless as memory, he laced his fingers into hers.

"Let's rest," he said when they returned.

She walked him to her bed, watched him pull a black turtleneck over thick, blond curls, slide off each black sock and shoe. His easy hands moved with surety and grace, the same way they coaxed the strings of a guitar, the same way they slid along her warm and pulsing places. Those spirals against his brow begging to be touched, his full-shaped mouth, that classic nose, he looked far more innocent than his years.

"Lie with me," he said. He smoothed the sheet. He beckoned her.

Making love with him was vast. It lifted her beyond her self, beyond the night. It seeded stars. She'd waited months to share a day with him, an hour, a caress—this man who used impermanence of an illusionary world as his excuse.

"Now is all there is," he said. "And it is real. And then it's not."

Yet he wrote her letters she could save, thick with layered words on smooth white paper marked by his illusionary hand. Words as lush and warm as down. Words that could sustain at least a part of her through seasoned stretches of too real time.

In morning light they lay, still joined, close as air, a mass of limbs and hair. Damp and full and shining. He hugged her, kissed her brow. Rhythmically, he played his fingers up and down her arm, as if her arm had strings. She thought she'd die of loving him.

"I need to call Marie," he said.

She knew about Marie. Knew that he flew in and out of lives upon the current of a whim. He was an eagle. He had to soar above a tethered world. He'd told her this in summer, atop a mountain, so she would understand.

"An eagle grounded is an awkward thing," he'd said. "It needs its wings. It needs the sky to feel its grace."

"Eagles mate for life," she'd said.

Two seasons later, still flying solo, the air beneath his wings was thin.

"I have to see Marie," he said.

Marie, who'd told him things were best kept grounded. Marie, a complication.

"I don't want to, but I need to see her. At least briefly. While I'm here," he said.

"It dishonors both of you to be where you don't want to be, to do what you don't want to do."

He didn't want to hear those words.

"You can use the phone downstairs," she said. She tried to be magnanimous, re-arranged her hair. She thought about impermanence, contemplated what was real and what was true and if they were the same.

Minutes later, he returned.

"I had to tell her that I just arrived," he said. "I had to say I wasn't staying here tonight." He pressed his hand against his brow as if to stop an ache.

"Lies can make a person ill," she said.

She felt ephemeral. Too insubstantial to be owned by him as someone he desired, as one with whom he chose to spend the night.

"I'm sorry. I didn't know what else to say," he said. "It became complicated. I won't be seeing her this time."

She didn't ask him why. She didn't want to know. Instead, she let him pull her toward him, smooth her cheek, reassure her with his touch.

"Now is all there is," he said. "And it is real."

Her mind imagined other beds in other nows made real by him. She let them fade. She felt for current meaning in his words, reached for truth in his caress, searched his eyes, where lies can't hide.

And she believed him.


It's half-way into spring and he is on his way to her again. Soon she'll look into his resurrected face. In public, he'll be cautious with his words, careful not to hold her hand. But then, when they're alone, he'll curl his length around her, kiss her with a tenderness that makes her weep, wake her sweetly in the night. He'll sing his poetry and run a bluesy riff on his guitar, contemplate absurdity and make her laugh. And when it's time to go, he'll ask again why things must always be so complicated. He'll promise next time not to wait so long.

# ABOUT THE AUTHOR

Rachelle Rogers is a poet, writer, and author of *A Love Apart*, a novel, and *Rare Atmosphere*, a memoir. She lives in Asheville, NC.

Visit her website at www.rachellerogers.com